Rachel & Annie

Rachel & Annie

A novel

Paul Seifert, M.D.

Authors Choice Press
San Jose New York Lincoln Shanghai

Rachel & Annie
A novel

Authors Choice Press
an imprint of iUniverse.com, Inc.

For information address:
iUniverse.com, Inc.
5220 S 16th, Ste. 200
Lincoln, NE 68512
www.iuniverse.com

ISBN: 0-595-19358-7

Printed in the United States of America

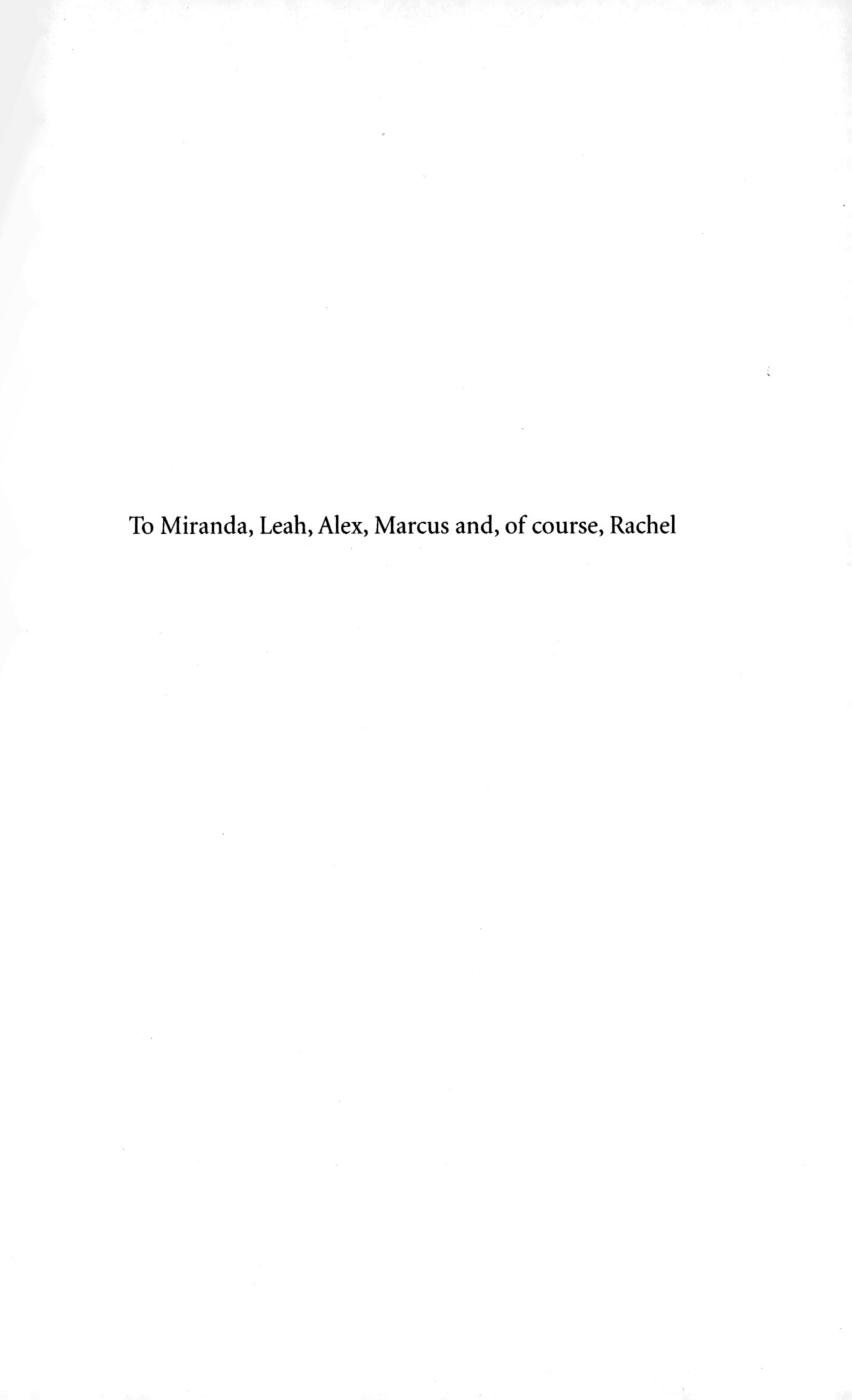
To Miranda, Leah, Alex, Marcus and, of course, Rachel

"There are in the end three things that last: faith, hope, and love, and the greatest of these is love."

I Corinthians 13

PROLOGUE

Note to the reader: a glossary of nautical terms is appended to the novel

A United States Coast Guard Search and Rescue helicopter, the *Pequod*, had been dispatched from its command post at the air station on Cape Cod. This latest mission was the *Pequod's* third since an unexpectedly severe late summer storm had decimated the New England coast. The heavy weather had been raging unabated for 36 hours.

The *Pequod's* mission was being coordinated from the Coast Guard Central Command Post at Southwest Harbor on Mount Desert Island in Maine. The aircraft was responding to a weakening signal from an *EPIRB*, an emergency position indicating radio beacon. The blips had been picked up by an aircraft flying over the Gulf of Maine. The *EPIRB* signal position was 44°, 0.2' North and 67°, 51.2' West, bearing 134° from Baker Island Light, which placed the distress location about 20 miles offshore.

Aboard the *Pequod* were five experienced Coast Guard personnel. The pilot, Lieutenant David "Zeke" Campbell, had flown rescue missions for a mobile hospital unit in Saudi Arabia. The co-pilot was Lieutenant Junior Grade Mike Benson. The crew aft included three petty officers. Dick Foster was the flight mechanic. His primary responsibility was operation of the *Pequod's* hoist. The radio operator was Diane Keeler. Petty Officer Keeler would maintain the flight log during the mission and would report the *Pequod's* constantly monitored position to the Southwest Harbor command station. The third person aft was Jack Cushing, the rescue swimmer. Cushing was prepared to haul the *Pequod's* array of emergency equipment into the sea, if the situation warranted his entry into the water.

The *Pequod* was flying into a stiff 35 knot nor'wester, with gusts still climbing into the high 40's. Visibility was less than half a mile. Mike Benson estimated the seas running below the chopper at 12-16 feet, so the pick-up—if there was to be one—was not going to be easy.

There had been no *Mayday* broadcasts from the vicinity of the unidentified distress signal. This meant that whoever was out there had either experienced a major power failure with loss of radio capability, or that the crew had abandoned ship and was adrift in a survival raft.

Campbell, Benson, and the rest of the crew had been in similar situations before. None of the *Pequod's* crew wanted to think about a more sobering possibility. There might not be anyone left alive to rescue. Occasionally, the crew of the *Pequod* encountered nothing at the end of a chase like this but a ghost ship, emitting an *EPIRP* signal, but bereft of crew. Considering the risk the *Pequod's* personnel were incurring by flying in such conditions, the possibility of this last contingency was disconcerting indeed.

"Command, this is the *Pequod*, over," Diane Keeler said into her microphone.

"Roger, *Pequod*, read you loud and clear, over."

"We must be less than ten minutes from target position," Petty Officer Keeler affirmed, "but we have zero, repeat zero, visual or consistent radar contact, over."

"Roger. Command standing by, out."

Mike Benson, the *Pequod's* co-pilot, peered into the murk. He could see little, other than an endless expanse of massive swells, breaking seas, spindrift, and spray. Benson had always been impressed by the desolate loneliness of the North Atlantic in a storm. The seascape below the chopper was almost surrealistic. The energy and strange undulating motion of the ocean was arresting, but forbidding. He had to convince himself at times like these that the sea was not haunted. He felt certain that he could make out strange shapes in the troughs of the endless waves, as if the North Atlantic were bringing up its dead. Mike Benson kept such conjectures strictly to himself.

"I have something on radar at 020°," Zeke Campbell exclaimed, breaking Benson's reverie. "Look sharp, Mike."

Benson could not make visual contact immediately, but then he saw an object in the waves ahead.

"Hey, Zeke, looks like we have a yacht!"

An RV, a recreational vessel, was the last thing the crew of the *Pequod* had expected. But the stricken vessel was a yacht, all right. Mike Benson estimated her length at 45 feet.

"Command, this is the *Pequod*," Benson said into his helmet microphone. "We have a sailor out here. She's adrift under bare poles, over."

The vessel was laboring badly in the substantial seas. She was taking green water on deck, but she appeared to be standing to it, with only a slight list to starboard.

"Can you make out a name, *Pequod*, over?" the command post requested.

Benson found it hard to fix his binoculars with the buffeting the *Pequod* was experiencing.

"Looks like the *Anna* something," Benson responded. "I can't copy the entire name, over."

"Any signs of life, over?"

"Not so far," Zeke Campbell said soberly.

"Wait a minute," Mike Benson said. "I think I see somebody at the companionway hatch. Looks like a kid to me. What do you think, Zeke?"

"Command, we're going in for a better look," Lieutenant Campell announced.

"The *Pequod* maneuvered into position closer to the disabled vessel. The crew of the chopper could see that she was cutter rigged, a canoe stern double ender. She looked well equipped, which was more than could be said for some RVs the *Pequod's* crew had encountered in similar circumstances.

"Yeah, the individual aboard is a kid all right," Lieutenant Campbell relayed to the command post. "Looks like a girl to me, maybe ten or twelve years old, over."

Captain Arthur Strickland, the Search and Rescue Mission Commander for the flight patched into the chopper.

"*Pequod*, this is Strickland. Any thoughts, people?"

Diane Keeler had been trying to raise the vessel on all possible radio frequencies, but with no success."

"We have a problem here, Captain," she spoke into her mike. "Their radios are either nonfunctional or the kid aboard doesn't know how to use them."

"She's life-jacketed and harnessed," Zeke Campbell added. "She looks fairly stable to me, Art, so I don't think she'll panic and go into the water, but there appears to be no way of finding out who else is aboard without sending Jack into the water. I'm hesitant to set a basket down for the kid without knowing whether she can handle the static electricity, over."

Without proper grounding on the surface vessel, the cables from the *Pequod's* evacuation baskets could seriously shock the occupants of the disabled ship. The instinct to grab the basket or cable without first allowing contact with the deck of the sailboat could prove fatal to the young girl aboard.

"Any chance of setting your aircraft down out there?" Captain Strickland asked.

Although the *Pequod* was an amphibious aircraft and had the capability of landing on the surface of the ocean, Zeke Campbell thought better of that option, given the sea state at the pickup site.

"We must be running some 16 footers out here, Art." "I'm not sure a set down would be a good idea. You are going to have to dispatch a surface vessel to haul the RV into port anyway, over."

"Roger, *Pequod*," Captain Strickland acknowledged. "Stand by while I get some things going from this end. What's your fuel status, Zeke?"

"Figuring in the trip home with the wind at our tail, we can sit out here approximately three hours, over." Zeke Campbell replied.

"Roger that, *Pequod*. Stand by."

The helicopter was hovering a few hundred feet from the disabled vessel. The girl aboard had stopped waving frantically and seemed to be monitoring events from the companionway in a state of relative calm. She had returned a thumb's up sign from Jack Cushing. Co-pilot Benson had been able to get a copy on the vessel's name. She was the *Anna Livia*. The command station ran a computer check on her and relayed out to the *Pequod* that the vessel was of American registry. The *Anna Livia* was a U.S. Coast Guard documented vessel owned by one Thomas O'Connor, whose listed address was one of the mail forwarding services that cruising yachtsmen occasionally use.

"Zeke, it's a go on Cushing's drop," Arthur Strickland said authoritatively. "We have the cutter *Grand Manan* en route out of Southwest Harbor. She's a 44-foot steel hull making 15 knots over the ground in the seas she's encountering. Her estimated time of arrival at your position is about an hour and forty minutes. We'll put a fire under her tail and see if she can better that, over."

"Roger, we copy," said Mike Benson.

The crew aft now went into action. Considering the conditions, the drop was effected smoothly. Petty Officer Cushing was lowered to the surface of the sea. After a few anxiety-provoking near misses in the swells, he had been able to board the *Anna Livia*.

Communicating with the *Pequod* via handheld VHF radio, the swimmer reported in.

"*Pequod*, this is Cushing. Do you copy, over?"

"Roger, Jack," Diane Keeler responded. "Read you loud and clear. What have you got down there?"

"From the looks of the mess, they must have taken a lightning strike. The batteries are blown and the electronics aboard are cooked. We have a med-evacuation situation. There's an old man aboard who is pretty banged up. He's dehydrated and has a chest injury of some kind. I'm going to start an I.V. Over."

"Roger, copy that," Mike Benson said. "We'll patch a call through Southwest Harbor to *Eastern Maine Medical Center* to alert them to expect some business. What's your estimate of the guy's condition?"

"Definitely critical," Cushing said. "I doubt he's going to make it."

"Roger that. What about the kid, over?"

"She tells me she's the old guy's granddaughter," Petty Officer Cushing replied. "She's a little upset, Mike, but she's O.K. otherwise. There isn't anybody else aboard, over."

"Did they have any man over boards?" Mike Benson asked.

"No, according to the kid, there was nobody else aboard. The kid and her grandfather were the entire crew."

"So what the hell were they doing out here?" Zeke Campbell asked, his voice betraying irritation.

"According to the kid," Jack Cushing responded, "they were sailing down from Nova Scotia so she could get back to school."

Impressively, the *Grand Manan* arrived in just under ninety minutes. Her crew supported the medical evacuation of the injured man. The rescue mission directed to the *Anna Livia* proceeded quickly from that point. Complying with what she said had been her grandfather's explicit instructions, the young girl—who said her name was Rachel—opted to stay with the ship.

Because of confusion and delirium, much of what was happening made little sense to Thomas O'Connor. He was aware of the presence of strangers aboard his boat. He realized he was being moved. The roar of what could only be helicopter rotor blades convinced him, during lucid intervals, that he had been strapped into an evacuation basket.

As he was lifted off the deck of the *Anna Livia*, Tom O'Connor felt that he was probably dying. In another brief moment of mental clarity, he was afforded a heart-rending view of his ship, as she lay floundering and wind swept in the swells below him. Helpless himself, he was being drawn away from her.

O'Connor recalled other views of *Annie* from even greater heights, when he and his wife, Anna, had stood together on bluffs or crags peering down with pride and admiration at their beloved ship lying at anchor below them. He was wrenched by the realization that he had now lost both of them, his wife and his ship.

Tom O'Connor would not be standing proudly in the cockpit when Rachel brought the *Anna Livia* into port. There would be no graceful entry under full sail this time. They had been at sea together for 22 years, he and his boat. For the first time in her life, the *Anna Livia* would limp into some unknown harbor ignominiously under tow.

Tom O'Connor sensed that he was moving extremely rapidly over the surface of the sea. His heartbeat seemed synchronized with the throbbing drone of the helicopter's rotor blades. His consciousness ebbed and his awareness of his present circumstances faded slowly. Before his eyes, the events of his past began to take the stage like scenes in a play of dreams.

Part I

Annie

Chapter One

As the rescue helicopter, the *Pequod*, continued its droning flight back to the mainland, Tom O'Connor remembered an afternoon he had knelt in the sand digging clams on a solitary North Atlantic beach. As the image solidified in his imagination, the scene became real, as if the events of his past were happening again.

Straightening momentarily, Tom massaged the stiffening muscles of his back. He then returned to the task at hand, the digging up of New England quahogs. He plunged his clam rake into the soft sand where a group of air holes and a single geyser betrayed the presence of the delectably edible creatures residing below. The clam rake efficiently separated clams from the wet sand that encased them.

"Three, four—that made an even three dozen, more than enough," he thought.

Placing the last of his catch into a small bucket, he straightened again. Slinging the rake over his shoulder, he ambled over to the saltwater wash that connected a small tidal basin with the belly of the surrounding sea.

Tom thought of himself as an old man, perhaps the oldest man in the state of Maine that day. He stood for a moment, his eyes scanning the quietude of the deserted beach. His attention fixed briefly on the slow dance of the Spartina grass in the salt marsh at the basin's edge. The evening breeze off Penobscot Bay played gently upon the slender reeds. Musical refrains began to echo through Tom's mind, half-remembered passages from Mozart or Bach.

Another hunter was at work in the sky above the beach. Tom peered skyward, his keen eye absorbing the antics of a shearwater. The bird, suspended in midair on ungainly flapping wings, suddenly dropped in a limp, but majestic free fall to the surface of the sea and then rose again, passing overhead in a smooth arc. The great bird's prey was twitching impotently within its beak.

Tom knelt in the sand again and began the ritualistic washing of his clams in the rushing stream of the tidal wash. The smell of the sea wrack exposed by the falling tide pleasantly assailed his nostrils. He worked on in solitude, his mind fading into an unspoken communion with his surroundings.

When the washing of freshly dug quahogs was completed, he rose nimbly to his feet. Hefting his gear and a bucket of clams as sand free as he cared to make them, he retraced his steps along the western shoreline of Big White Island. He was headed back to the place he had beached his dinghy.

Tom O'Connor never tired of walking the beaches and tidal flats at the edge of the ocean. His fascination was as keen now as it had been years before when he had first trudged the coastlines of Nova Scotia. He had always been mesmerized by the intricate details of the silently contested battleground where the land meets the sea.

The shoreline of Big White Island led from the sand flats past a sharply contrasting granite escarpment where the sea continues to gnaw endlessly at the ancient rock. Huge boulders, white and piebald from the reticulations of a surface coat of lichen, thrust skyward from the ocean's edge. Trees growing at the very edge of the escarpment leaned precariously in the direction of the sea. Many had fallen to the beach already and were transmuting slowly into driftwood.

As he made his way in the direction of his dinghy, Tom stopped from time to time to extract some article of human jetsam, a plastic beer can holder or a styrofoam cup, from the pristine beach. He placed these objects in a plastic garbage bag he carried hooked to his belt. He did this with commitment and resignation, but without the anger about the pollution of the sea he had felt in earlier years. The anger had done little good, either for him or the ocean. He had found it best to simply do his part, ineffectual as his efforts undoubtedly were.

Tom made his way past a singular group of trees that lay fallen amid the rocks. The gnarled roots, stripped of their bark by the incessant wind and waves, had assumed tortured, almost humanoid configurations. They looked like strangely sculpted figures with polished and twisted limbs grasping in anguish at some object not readily seen. They reminded him of the mute victims of some great conflagration, like the castings of bodies he and Anna had once seen at Pompeii. The engaging figures seemed at one with the shells, the bleached skeletons of fish, and the softer dead things—a sea bird and the innumerable beached jelly fish—that lay about.

The granite escarpment gave way at the north end of the island to another section of sandy beach, again festooned with elegant patches of wiry Spartina grass. Tom trudged with more difficulty over the slippery sand until he found a firmer footing in the shale nearer the water's edge. The force of the bimonthly spring tides and the wind had driven the shale and sand into crests, the summits of which were capped with a luxuriant growth of ground cover. The sun, now lowering in the northwestern sky and filling the gap between Big White and Garden Islands, caught the plant forms in its glow, electrifying the beach with sparkles of an iridescent crimson hue. Light appeared to be emanating from a myriad of miniscule lanterns all along the beach. Tom knew such sights are elusive, absent on most days, appearing only in consequence of some unpredictable atmospheric balance. The old sailor savored the intense unworldly beauty of the phenomenon.

Passing on and nearing the spot where his dinghy lay beached, Tom scrambled up a sand knoll peppered with clusters of sea grass. From the perspective of the summit, he took in the vista of the surrounding archipelago of islands.

The engrossing scene before him was highlighted by the mirrored surface of the sea, which sparkled in the waning sunlight like a vast track of diamonds. Sun-painted clouds were hanging low on the eastern horizon. A little farther on, Tom caught his first glimpse of the *Anna Livia.* She lay at anchor, within a brilliant aureole of light, in the gap between Big White and Little White Islands. His ship seemed suspended in stately majesty, as if she was riding above the surface of the water. Tom stopped in his tracks. Twenty-two years, he mused reflectively, and she still affected him that way. Coming or going, he always had to stop a moment or two to wistfully take in her lines.

When he reached the dinghy, Tom quickly buried the garbage he had collected from the beach in the sand above the high water mark. Then he dropped to the ground and stretched his body along a pocket in the warm sand. As was his custom, whenever possible, he watched the sun set behind the striking profile of Vinalhaven Island.

"Amen-Ra entering Amenti, the Egyptian realm of the dead," he mused aloud, as the setting sun in the next few moments painted a masterpiece in the sky. "Red sky at night, sailor's delight," Tom murmured softly.

When the celestial display had nearly ended, Tom removed his sandals and launched the dinghy into the gentle ebb and flow of the surf. With steady strokes of the oars, he began to row out to his ship. Tom O'Connor never rowed in the conventional manner, with his back to the bow of the dinghy. He loved to ogle the larger vessel as he approached her, so he sat facing the stern of the dinghy and pushed, rather than pulled, at the oars.

Tom traced the stately lines of the *Anna Livia* as he approached her in the twilight. A crescent moon was just rising in the east. His boat was a Hans Christian 38, a double ender, cutter rigged, and nearly 50 feet in overall length from the tip of her 9-foot bowsprit to her stern pulpit. She was a sea kindly sailing vessel and had logged thousands of sea miles since her commissioning in the month of April twenty-two years before. The name officially recorded in her documentation papers and stenciled at both stern quarters was the *Anna Livia*, "Anna" with a soft "a", but years before her name had been shortened to the simpler, *Annie*. Except, that is, over the ship-to-shore radio, when she was always the *Anna Livia, Anna Livia, Anna Livia*, Whiskey, Tango, X-ray 2773.

Tom came alongside and secured the dinghy for boarding. "Teak's about due," he reflected, as he climbed aboard over the wooden cap rail.

"Lotta teak!" he said aloud.

Tom smiled as he repeated a familiar litany.

"But I live aboard, you see. It's not so bad, cleaning and oiling teak. Kind of like mowing grass or pruning rose bushes."

Tom followed the seductive rise of her sheer line, as *Annie's* teak decks and cap rail rose to an aesthetically satisfying completion at her bowsprit.

"Sure wouldn't want to have to take care of all that teak!" he said.

Memories of times and persons long gone swirled through Tom's head like the silent creatures flying in the moonlight as he toured *Annie's* foredeck. As was his custom, he readjusted the nip in the nylon shock line rigged to the all chain anchor rode, making certain all was secure for the coming night. He then checked his shore transits, assuring himself that *Annie* had not dragged since he had set her anchor several hours earlier. The weather was settled, no trouble in sight. The stillness of the evening was interrupted only by the mournful cry of a solitary loon in the distance.

"Tom made his way aft and then stopped for a moment at the companionway hatch, surveying the twilight sky as he prepared to go below. A refrain entered his mind. "A ship, an isle, a sickle moon with few but splendid stars. The mirrors of the shining sea are strewn with silver bars."

Unable to place the source of the lines, Tom directed his attention to the sky.

"First star," he muttered, "*Arcturus* in *Bootes*. Damned fine star, old *Arcturus*."

Tom O'Connor peered up at the brilliant star, *Arcturus*, the bear keeper, fourth brightest and first named star in the heavens, twenty million miles in diameter, moving faster through space than any other first magnitude star in the sky, except *Alpha Centaurus* and *Rigil Kentaurus*. Tom recycled the strange lore of stars in his thoughts and then he gave thanks for many a useful sight taken of *Arcturus* in *Bootes* by sextant upon the lonely offshore reaches of the sea.

Chapter Two

Cozy light from a brass trawler lantern suspended from the overhead suffused *Annie's* saloon with a warm glow amid which were brilliant highlights, flashing intermittently as the ship rolled to a gentle swell. These illuminations came from nautical artifacts, a barograph encased in mahogany and glass, a polished sextant box, a collection of gleaming copper cookware, and a bronze compression post glossed to a mirrored finish. This last object lent vital support to the vessel's mast.

A painting, Rogier van der Weyden's *Portrait of a Young Woman*, adorned the main bulkhead, which separated *Annie's* main saloon from the heads and forecastle up forward. The copper cookware was mounted to an aft bulkhead that defined the ship's galley. Behind this bulkhead was the aft stateroom, where Tom O'Connor spent his nights alone.

Tom stood in the galley steaming his clams. The smell of the simmering quahogs mingled with a faint scent of kerosene from the lamp and the vague mustiness of an aging ship, bringing to his nostrils the subtle aroma of familiarity and home.

The old sailor's repast, served at the saloon table a few moments later, was simple fare—clam chowder, complemented by a few crusts of drying bread, from which the bluish-green intrusions of mold had been surgically excised.

Having eaten, Tom selected a book from an adjacent shelf, one fitted with lee rails to secure its contents from the heeling moment of a ship under sail. The book was *The Liturgy of the Hours,* for the 12th through 32nd weeks of ordinary time. Turning to a page marked with a scarlet ribbon, Tom O'Connor read the evening prayers for June 21st of a year that had faded into the past decades ago.

Tom was not a priest, but he liked to think of himself as reading along communally with priests. He could feel them out there somewhere, his unseen spiritual brothers, as he formed the words of the evening office silently with his lips. He had given thought to entering a monastery at one time, perhaps to become a Trappist monk like Thomas Merton, whose books Tom had avidly read. But he had not become a monk. He had not been able to relinquish his love affair with the sea.

"Oh, I have loved thee, wanton ocean," Tom mused. He had settled instead for a monastery of the mind.

Tom O'Connor supplemented his liturgical reading with five obligatory pages from *Ulysses.* As was his custom, he continuously reread in turn each of James Joyce's major works. He had been reading Joyce's books for nearly thirty years.

His evening readings completed, Tom was suddenly overcome by fatigue. He sat quietly, listening to the gentle slap of a halyard against *Annie's* mast, but having no inclination to go topsides and harden the rigging. The ship's clock had just struck six bells. The time was 11 P.M. He had some whippings and a few splices to do, but he could muster no enthusiasm for marlinspiking tonight.

Tom turned down the flame in the trawler lamp above his head until the light in the cabin became more dimly suffused. Out of the semidarkness at the edge of the circle of light cast by the lamp, the face of an angel appeared. The porcelain statue was mounted to a shelf attached to *Annie's* forward bulkhead.

Tom surveyed the details of that familiar face as his loneliness descended like an incoming fog to engulf his spirit in melancholy pain. Unlike a mounting sea or a building wind, he knew there was little he could do to fend off this disconcerting feeling when it appeared. Activity helped when he was at sea, as did the light of day, but at night—if he was not particularly vigilant—this most singular discomfort would inevitably return, as it had on this night.

Tom O'Connor closed and then opened his misted eyes. The woman sitting across from him on the settee was dressed in sweats and an old foul weather jacket, but even in such casual attire, he found her beautiful.

"I'll love you until the ocean is folded and hung up somewhere to dry," he said softly.

This woman was smiling at Tom O'Connor, a smile of gentle approbation. Her relatively youthful appearance compared to his own pained him. How would she be able to want him, accept him, when, or if?

"I suppose I'll put into Camden tomorrow for mail," he said aloud, his voice breaking audibly.

"Yes," her wistful expression of approval said, "yes."

Chapter Three

Tom O'Connor turned out of his bunk at 6:00 A.M., as *Annie's* clock chimed four bells. He brewed a pot of fresh coffee and set a flame beneath the chowder left from the night before. Chomping some saltine crackers, Tom checked his course line for Camden on a frayed chart of Penobscot Bay. Between forays into his coastal pilot and tide tables, he managed to put together a breakfast and lunch. Then he read his morning office.

By six bells, Tom was topsides. As promised by the crimson sky of the previous evening, the weather was clear. There was a chill in the air and the wind here in the lee of Big White Island was light, but all signs betokened a perfect day. Tom toured the decks of his ship, swabbing the salt spray from her teak with a yacht mop soaked in the morning dew. The tide was down, as predicted by the tide tables for this date, time, and place. The smell of sea wrack was heavy in Tom's nostrils, despite the light early morning air.

Tom stripped the covers from *Annie's* tanbark sails, and then liberated the helm from its canvas pedestal cover. The beautiful brass cathedral compass mounted at the steering pedestal gleamed smartly in the sunlight. Giving the white granite rocks and ragged trees of the stunningly beautiful White Island archipelago a last wistful look from his vantage point at *Annie's* helmsman's seat, Tom rose to his feet to begin the process of getting his ship underway.

His progress forward in the direction of the anchor rode was arrested, however. The woman of the previous evening was sitting relaxed in the cockpit. The admonishing expression on her face directed Tom's attention to the surrounding water.

He made a feeble protest, but the woman's countenance conveyed the fact that she would brook no resistance.

"Okay!" he said aloud, expressing some irritation. He stripped quickly, muttering as he fussed with his clothing.

Tom O'Connor's body was lean and wiry, his muscles firm from season after season at sea. This had not always been the case. When he was in the profession, he had been flabby, fatigued most of the time, and morbidly preoccupied with death. Now, at age 64, Tom's body was not that of an old man. Except for silver gray hair and a beard of similar hue, his body belied its age. Still, Tom felt that he was old—an old man of the sea. Stepping briskly to *Annie's* cap rail, he plunged over the side.

Breaking the surface of the frigid water, Tom vigorously massaged his armpits and crotch—characteristically, he had forgotten his soap—before climbing back aboard up the rope ladder that hung amidships from *Annie's* hull. He vigorously massaged the water from his tingling skin and then donned his sweats and oiled wool sweater, sniffing cautiously at his pits as he did so.

"You never would sleep with a man who didn't bathe at least once a day, would you?" he asked aloud.

A bemused expression on the woman's face playfully acknowledged this profound truth.

His ablutions in the bone chilling waters of the Gulf of Maine completed, Tom O'Connor proceeded in earnest with getting the *Anna Livia* underway. Making his way to the starboard mast pulpit, he released the main halyard and winched the big tanbark sail about a third of the way toward the masthead.

Adroitly moving forward, he cranked at *Annie's* windlass until the hook left the bottom. *Annie's* bow drifted off to port as the anchor was weighed. Leaving the hook trailing in the water to free it of mud and a few recalcitrant strands of kelp, Tom returned to the mast pulpit and quickly raised the mainsail to the masthead. *Annie* heeled to port a degree or two and began to move down the slot between the islands toward the open waters of Penobscot Bay, trailing the dinghy behind her. The wind was right for a gentle reach at about a knot, so Tom locked the helm and went back forward to stow the anchor in its roller on the bowsprit. Returning to the mast, he cranked up the genoa and smaller staysail.

The headsails picked up the southwest breeze blowing in off the southern tip of Big White Island and the *Anna Livia* came to life. Heeling now fifteen degrees to port, she began to surge forward with power and authority. Tom had to make a few short tacks as the wind came bow on rounding the extreme southern tip of Big White Island, but in no time *Annie* was tracking off to the northwest on course to Camden, which was about 12 nautical miles ahead.

Tom O'Connor thrilled to the occasion as *Annie's* motion livened. This was going to be one of those perfect sailing days, the kind impossible to tire of at sea, no matter how many of them you manage to experience in a lifetime. Tom checked the set of *Annie's* sails, as she swept safely past the shoals awash off Medric Rock. *Annie* was a tractable beast, he thought to himself, when she was fed, and old *Annie* ate the wind.

Tom leaned gently into the helm and directed his craft over the crests of the waves into the troughs from where she rose again smartly, surging forward into the seas. From the countless hours he had sat or stood at *Annie's* bowsprit while underway, the old sailor knew how her sleek bow was slicing though the water with incredible power. He had often been in awe, from that perspective up forward, of the tremendous forces at play in a vessel working to weather under sail.

Tom glanced over his shoulder at the silhouette of Vinalhaven Island as the landmass receded slowly off the starboard quarter. Ahead, the Camden hills were lost in a sparkling mantle of radiant sunlight. The wind was now rushing into his left ear and Tom's eyes were tearing in the freshening breeze as *Annie* heeled more to starboard and leapt forward in response to a gust. The first rogue wave broke over the bow and swept aft along the decks to the midships scuppers. Four porpoises appeared, their sleek backs breaking the swells in unison off the port side of the bow.

Tom leaned more firmly into *Annie's* helm as the wind stiffened. He rode on with her as she swallowed up the sea at a breathtaking seven knots. The rhythmic motion of a ship on the sea is one of those unique human experiences that can bring about a state of timeless ecstasy. For Tom O'Connor, time indeed began to slow and the outside world began to dissolve into a miraculous melding of sailor, ship, wind, and wave. On this glorious day, Tom O'Connor was an aging sailor who had not yet fallen from grace with the sea.

The Graves, the rocks southeast of the entrance to Camden, would come into view only too soon. But until then, this event, this process was all that mattered in the world. This was to be a great sail.

Tom O'Connor peered longingly into the face of his companion and winked. Anna's familiar smile wrenched at his heart, but of course she agreed. This was to be one of the greatest of sails.

CHAPTER FOUR

As the *Anna Livia* drew abeam of the green flasher mounted atop the rocks called the Graves outside Camden, Tom O'Connor dropped her genoa. *Annie* slowed perceptibly, but she continued to make good way until she had skirted the northeast corner of Curtis Island, where Tom doused her staysail.

Flying her main alone, *Annie* effected her usual proud and stately entry into the harbor at Camden, Maine. Tom steered his ship into Sherman's Cove, the bight at the northeast corner of what is called Camden's outer harbor. Just outside the field of privately owned mooring buoys, Tom brought *Annie's* bow hard on to the wind. He locked her wheel and skipped up to the mast and let her main halyard fly. As the mainsail flailed in the wind, *Annie* lost power and forward momentum. By the time she began to settle back with the wind, Tom had reached her bowsprit and had dropped her hook in a series of deft maneuvers facilitated by years of practice. He paid out some of the anchor rode and then returned to the mast pulpit. He partially raised and backwinded the mainsail to set the hook. Within minutes, the *Anna Livia* lay quietly at anchor.

Tom bagged and covered his sails and then spent a few minutes organizing things below decks. Two brass candelabras and a trio of small porcelain angels were part of his collection of treasured artifacts, impractical as it was to have such items aboard a sailing vessel. He retrieved the objects from the sanctuaries amid the sail bags and bedding where they had spent a safe passage protected from the rough shocks of the sea and returned them to their accustomed places in *Annie's* saloon.

At one time, the most treasured of Tom O'Connor's special things had been his wife's musical jewelry box, which played the *Canon in D* of Johann Pachelbel. In recent years, he had been unable to bear the despair engendered by the sight of this once precious object. He had wrapped it carefully in plastic and stowed it forward in a storage compartment.

His ship now secure, Tom boarded his dinghy and rowed into shore. Rowing now in conventional fashion he was able to watch *Annie* as she receded into the distance. With firm strokes at the oars, he rounded Eaton Point and made his way between the mooring buoys to the public landing area at the head of the inner harbor. There, he came ashore and secured his tender against predators and adventuresome small boys.

Tom's first order of business was to place a call to his mail forwarding service. He asked the service to send any letters being held for him to the Camden Post Office, care of general delivery. Tom was informed his package would reach Maine within three days. He knew he would not have accumulated much mail in the three months since his last pickup. Most of it would be dry financial statements concerning the annuities and dividends that comprised his substantial retirement income. There was always the chance of a letter or note from his daughter, Claire, to whom he wrote on occasion, in the intervals between the more convenient phone calls.

The small park at the head of the harbor was teeming with activity, since the Maine tourist season was now in full swing. Tom spent an hour on one of the benches watching the ebb and flow of humanity, then he began to retrace the walks he and Anna had taken during their many visits to this favored port town. He made his way past the Down East Trading Company and then along the eastern rim of the inner harbor out to the docks of Wayfarer Marine. Inspecting other boats sometimes led to the discovery of a useful item that could be adapted to *Annie's* rig, but the junket on this particular day proved unrewarding. Tom was afforded a reassuring glimpse of the *Anna Livia*, however, as she lay secure and unmolested in Sherman's Cove.

Tom returned to the head of harbor, where his eyes respectfully dissected the lines and the rigging of a windjammer or two. Next he made his way to the west along Maine Route One, which runs through the center of town, and then out past the shore facilities that line the western rim of Camden harbor. As he ambled past places that he and Anna had once visited together, he was beset by a sense of bittersweet nostalgia. The gentle chime of a church bell seemed to echo Anna's laugh or the sound of her voice. He seemed to see her in the shapes and forms of strangers moving ahead of him. He paused and stared wistfully at the diners in the *Water Front*, a restaurant he and Anna had frequented on occasion.

Craving no company, Tom O'Connor walked on for hours, his mind riveted to the past. He walked the familiar streets of Camden to no purpose until the mournful diaphone of foghorns began to instill the late afternoon air with warning of the approach of a mysterious white night in the middle of the day.

After picking up a sandwich at one of Camden's delicatessens, Tom returned to the head of the harbor, retrieved his dinghy, and rowed out to his ship against a rising tide and a flood of painful memories. The thickening air had softened *Annie's* silhouette by the time she came into view. Once aboard, Tom stood for a time at the bowsprit, watching the incoming fog slowly obliterate the town of Camden until all traces of a world outside the contained universe of his ship had been erased by the thickening mist.

Chapter Five

Tom O'Connor was not idle as he awaited the arrival of his mail. He spent much of his time aboard his boat engaged in the Sisyphean labor necessary to maintain the *Anna Livia* what she was, a small ship of transcendent beauty, a vessel apart from her sisters. Tom labored on his boat because of simple respect and love for an object of classical proportion and line that, at least in his view, was irrefutably alive.

One aspect of the *Anna Livia's* magnetism was kinetic and became fully expressed when she came to life with power and intensity on the sea. Yet another dimension of *Annie's* elegance was in contrast static, part of a Joycean esthetic that could arrest the mind of a beholder, leaving the observer in awe of the object beheld.

A sense of these things motivated Tom O'Connor to polish brass that would surrender to the corrosion of salt spray in days, to polish and oil teak that would fade from the ravages of weather and wear. Still, he worked on, waxing and rubbing his ship and its fittings with a great sense of purpose and privilege. To him had fallen the honor of dressing a great lady in all of her finery. Tom scoffed at those who take umbrage at the feminine qualities of certain ships.

As he sat in the cockpit greasing winches, whipping frayed rigging, or repairing his sails, admirers would often come by, circling *Annie* in dinghies as she lay in stately grace at anchor. Questions or comments would invariably follow.

"Beautiful boat you have there."

"What kind of vessel is she?"

"Been across the ditch?"

"Sure has a lot of teak!"

Tom O'Connor would respond politely with a word or two before withdrawing into the protective mantle of the task at hand.

Tom rowed back into shore frequently in the next few days. He hauled in a load of garbage and made a visit to *Clothes Care Unlimited* on Mechanic Street where he deposited his dirty laundry. He hiked out to *Merry Spring Nature Park* on Russel Avenue—one of Anna O'Connor's favorite places. On another occasion, he walked over to Rockport, a small but beautiful harbor a few miles to the west of Camden.

An observer encountering Tom O'Connor on one of his junkets might have been impressed by the disparity between the face and body of this man. The muscular body, draped simply in sweats and a T-shirt, appeared that of a man in the late summer of his life. Tom's step was light, even jaunty at times. But his face did not seem to fit this body. Tom O'Connor's face appeared much older, as though it might have been pasted on the wrong frame like an altered photograph.

Stringy gray hair, nearly shoulder length, crept in ragged strands from the rim of Tom's battered Greek fisherman's hat. The green eyes below the rim of this hat might have been intense, even piercing, had they been directed with any enthusiasm toward the external world.

Of Tom O'Connor's lower face, not much was to be seen. A beak-like nose and then a mass of scraggly hair surrounded a small delicate mouth, all but lost between his beard and moustache. Tom wore a gold stud earring, a gift from his wife on his fifty-second birthday.

More disturbing for many strangers than his appearance, however, was the fact that Tom O'Connor often appeared to be talking to himself as he ambled along. In fact, the half-completed sentences he uttered within hearing range of anyone passing by were not for him, but for Anna and no one else. His conversations with her were simply essential to his survival, leaving him little insight into the psychology of his aberration.

Like many of those who engage in conversations with the dead in public places, Tom O'Connor was more often than not judged harshly for his peculiar habit. Still, he paid not a wit of attention to the sometimes less than charitable reactions to his conversations with his soul mate, oblivious as he usually was to anyone else in his surroundings.

Tom generally spoke to Anna about persons or things shared during their lives together. From the moment of his wife's death, Tom O'Connor's life had ceased to move forward. He remained trapped in a past where Anna O'Connor still existed. He could project his mind into the future only far enough to predict the coming phases of the moon and the affect the resulting tides and currents might have on the operation of his boat. He sailed a repetitive circuit along the Atlantic coast from Nova Scotia to the Florida Keys, moving north or south as the seasons dictated.

Otherwise, Tom O'Connor no longer marked the slow passage time and he made no other plans for his future. His decision to dig New England quahogs on a sand flat in Maine was less related to his need of sustenance in the present than to his desire to share those clams again with Anna beneath the trawler lamp in *Annie's* cabin. Putting into Camden had not been related to any great interest he had in his mail. Rather, that particular harbor in Maine afforded him the opportunity to relive experiences there that he and Anna had shared. Only in this way could they be together, together again watching the placid ocean and the canopy of the midsummer sky.

On his second full day in Camden, Tom O'Connor walked north up Main Street in the early morning, turned left onto Route 52—known locally as "Mountain Street"—and then again to the right onto Megunticook Street. He was heading for the trail that led to the summit of Mount Battie. Once he had reached trail head, Tom charged up the ascending pathway with authority.

"Not breathing so hard as the last time we were here," he said aloud. "How about you?"

No, she was not breathing so hard this time either.

From the stone tower at the summit of Mount Battie, the view is spectacular. When Tom reached the crown of the hill, he stood for a moment surveying the vistas of Camden harbor nestled below. Vinalhaven Island lay to seaward, and more distantly Isle au Haut. These familiar landmarks emerged from the softening atmospheric distortion clinging to the base of the hills and the undulating edges of the sea.

"Do you remember the first time we climbed the trail to the fire tower on Blue Hill?' he asked, his voice strident with gleeful enthusiasm.

Tom laughed hardily, slapping the side of his knee.

"I'll never forget how afraid you were to climb any higher than the first level of that tower! 'I can see perfectly well from here,' you said. And me? Hell, I was scared to death too, but I never let on that I was. Too macho for honesty in those days, by God! Climbing that tower was nearly as bad as being winched to the masthead in a rolling sea!"

Tom laughed until tears filled his eyes.

Anna's expression was whimsically forgiving as she reluctantly removed her eyes from the seaboard far below and confronted him.

"You old coot," her face seemed to say, "Do you really think I didn't know how scared you were?"

Chapter Six

Tom O'Connor's knee slapping laugh ceased abruptly, as the vision of his wife dissipated into the vibrant distortions of the warm summer air. Alone again, he was suddenly overcome by listlessness. He ambled over to one of the scruffy pine trees that cling to the rocks at the summit of Mount Battie. He sat down on a bed of pine needles and dozed off. When he awoke, he ate the lobster roll he had brought with him to the summit, but with little relish for the food. The wind was soughing in the trees, a mournful sound that Anna O'Connor had always loved.

The present circumstances of Tom O'Connor's life had not been planned.

They had met in high school in the springtime of their lives, introduced by a cousin of his. The meeting had been for both of them, as it turned out, one of those singular electric encounters that people call love at first sight. Tom and Anna had sensed even when young that they had been graced with a mystical communion, as of kindred spirits who had not only fallen in love, but who had rediscovered one another. The intensity of those early feelings had never abated. Their relationship was destined to last forty-two years.

Until death do us part.

They had been lucky in love, he and Anna. They had married unconventionally early and had both struggled to make it through college. Professionally, he had gone into law. Anna had pursued a career in education and had become a professor of art history, specializing eventually in the Northern Renaissance works of the so-called Flemish Primitives. Together, they had made ridiculous amounts of money.

With the birth of their son two years after their marriage and the construction of the classic house in the suburbs, their lives seemed to have reached completion. Theirs was a good life, enviable without doubt. But for Tom O'Connor, at least, even then there had been intimations that it was not the life he really wanted to live.

The first crack in the crystal palace he and Anna had constructed for themselves had come with the death of their young son at the age of three. His had been a ruthless, unexpected death from meningitis, a devastating disease of unrelenting strength that had simply overwhelmed their small child.

The O'Connors had proved vulnerable to the vicissitudes of life after all. No one recovers from the loss of a small child. Twenty years later, they would mist up at the sight of anyone else's three-year-old son. They did follow well-intentioned counsel. Their second and last child, a little girl named Claire, had been born within a year.

And so the years had passed. All the while, Tom O'Connor was experiencing a vague, but growing sense of discontent. He had become a classic workaholic. He was soon a very successful lawyer, a lousy father, a marginal husband, and a physical wreck. He pushed his friendship with Anna to the limits. Fortunately for him, she stood by him through those dark and self-destructive years.

Even now, Tom O'Connor admitted there had never been a rational basis for his discontent. Professionally, he was envied, respected, even admired. To quote a colleague, "he had it made." All of the usual metaphors of success applied to him. He had tried to analyze his problem on his own. He had even sought professional help, but to no lasting benefit. Tom became convinced that his therapist secretly despised him. Tough as his son's death had been to accept, unresolved grief did not seem to explain the nagging sense of unrest he was feeling.

Tom recognized at times a sense of guilt about what was being done by people like him to the planet and those less fortunate than he was, but he also realized that he was incapable of closing his bank accounts, renouncing all wealth, and feeding the poor and homeless. He was only willing to part with a little of his ill gotten gains in the conventional fashion of the day, as tax deductible—always tax deductible—contributions to a worthy cause here and there.

But then events had reached a crisis just after Tom's fortieth birthday. His internist, who he had finally consulted at Anna's urging, had bluntly put his situation into perspective.

"You, Tom, are a heart attack looking for a place to happen! You should consider this visit a crossroads in your life."

And so it had proved to be.

Tom O'Connor had been informed that he was 25 pounds overweight, was drinking far too much, had high blood pressure, a cholesterol off the page, and a classic "type A personality." The only things going for him were the facts that he did not smoke and had not yet developed diabetes. He had always been aware that he had been dealt a bad genetic hand. Coronary disease was rampant on his mother's side of his family.

"You simply have to clean up your act, Tom, or it's going to be curtains for you and early widowhood for your wife," his physician had admonished. "Lose some weight, start an exercise program, and do something with your life besides generating huge sums of money or you are going to die, Tom. Why don't you take up sailing or something else as relaxing."

Tom and Anna O'Connor had of course taken up sailing. They had signed on for a live aboard, learn to sail course in Canada. From that first screaming reach down a wind swept, rock-strewn channel in the Georgian Bay with a reckless sloop in hot pursuit, Tom at least had been smitten by the sport. The O'Connors had followed up the course with a couple of crewed and then a bareboat charter in the Caribbean. Then, two years later, they had purchased the *Anna Livia*, a large first boat by conventional standards.

The big cutter had intimidated Tom at first, but he had learned to handle her moods and she seemed to diminish in size over the seasons. From the very moment he had stepped aboard, however, Tom O'Connor had been bitten by a desire to chuck it all and take the *Anna Livia* to sea.

Anna O'Connor was hesitant in the beginning. She was not so ready to abandon the nest or her career. Claire was only eleven and she did not really enjoy the boat. Tom didn't realize that a youngster approaching her teens doesn't always find much of interest on her parents' yacht. In Claire's view, sailing was boring, the boat was boring, life was boring. No doubt, her parents were particularly boring.

They did sail some together, despite Claire's reluctance, and they did have some terrific times. But Tom had not approached the situation correctly at first. He learned only later that a man should never confine a woman to the role of mate if he wants her sail with him with enthusiasm. Tom had tried to assume command in those early days. He had tried to do everything on the boat himself, to make all of the decisions.

Old Dave Gordon, the harbormaster down at the marina where Tom O'Connor began to spend more of his time alone, had eventually set Tom straight.

"You're going to lose those women, Tom, if you don't take care. I've seen it all a hundred times over. A man and his family get a boat and spend the first year or so on it together. He's fussing all the time, shouting orders, and generally mucking everything up. But he blames all of his mistakes on them, of course.

"Pretty soon, he's out here alone a lot, just like you, Tom. Either you get into single handed sailing, or you'll go through the usual sequence of sailing with the men and young boys until one day, there's another woman out here with you a few seasons down the line.

"These boats have wrecked more than their share of good marriages, believe me!"

Tom, heeding Dave's advice, had learned to single handle *Annie.* Then he began a concerted effort to woo Anna back into the fold. He developed a sailor's patience as he eased his wife back into all the phases of the operation of the boat. His efforts paid off. From a white-knuckled grip on *Annie's* helm, Anna O'Connor evolved to sailing one handed and in time to sailing with one foot on the wheel. About then, during the third season they had owned *Annie,* Anna O'Connor had become a sailor too. As might have been predicted, she became one hell of lot better sailor than her husband would ever be.

Professionally, Tom O'Connor's situation continued to deteriorate. Preoccupied, living only for the next cruise or free weekend, he survived on sheer will. He was convinced he was going to have a heart attack or stroke at any moment. In fairness, Tom truly believed that his family history and the circumstances of his life style had condemned him to an early demise. He was not morbidly preoccupied with death. But he was convinced that he would be lucky to reach sixty. He did not want to spend the last decade of his life making money and wasting precious time.

The sincerity of Tom's feelings eventually convinced Anna that early retirement might be best for both of them. As for Anna herself, she was convinced that she was going die a little old lady at the age of 93.

What had evolved to become an untenable situation at Tom's office was finally resolved after Claire left home to go to college. Tom O'Connor did retire early to cruise the Atlantic Coast. He was fifty years old the day he left.

Tom's colleagues in the law firm were skeptical.

"You'll get bored of it within six months, Tom," Jack Fitzgerald, his closest colleague at the office assured him. "What the hell can you possibly do sitting on a sailboat all day? You'll be back, good buddy!"

But Tom O'Connor had never gone back.

The real surprise about living full-time aboard the boat had been the way Anna warmed to the situation. She found the loss of the house less traumatic than he had anticipated. *Annie* quickly evolved from boat to home. There had been sacrifices, naturally, and most of these had been more stressful for Anna than for Tom. But co-skipper O'Connor had adapted to life at sea, despite the cramped space, dearth of an unlimited supply of hot running water, and room for only a limited wardrobe.

"Shoes, Tom," Anna O'Connor had lamented one day, "shoes are what I miss most. I'd have the whole boat swimming in pumps and heels, if there was room!"

"Thank God," Tom had muttered beneath his breath, "there is not enough room."

Cruising under sail had never been boring. What can you possibly do sitting on a sailboat all day? What a joke that one proved to be! The days literally flew by, filled with activity. Boat maintenance is a Sisyphean labor. Tom O'Connor's list of things to fix, scrub, or polish was never completed. Just when it appeared he might be finished with his tasks, two or three new items would break down. Still, both O'Connors soon realized that the expenditure of energy spent at boat maintenance is stimulating to the body and relaxing to the spirit, nothing like the effects of what passes for work in the professional arena.

Time was consumed with the navigation planning for the next passage, with laundry, and the stocking of provisions. Best of all, cruising opened aspects of the world that had neither of the O'Connors had experienced before.

Tom and Anna visited quaint harbor towns and ports, each unique, but each offering solace from the irrational rages that plague the sea. They became enamoured with the wildflowers of North America, which they identified, catalogued, and nurtured. They experienced days of good fortune in the sailor's lottery of the wind, when a fair passage quickly made warms the spirit like a good slug of rum on a brisk fall day. They labored at hard beats into the wind that test the endurance of ship and crew. They suffered torpid days when there is no wind at all and the ship sways like a true drunken sailor in the swells and the sails flog impotently. At such times, even the most diehard sailor curses Aeolus, the god of the wind, reluctantly pulls down the rags, and fires up the iron jib. On such days of merciless sun and zero wind, the flies would come, falling like the rebel angels to cover every square inch of the ship, until the blackened decks become a battlefield of insect carnage.

Tom O'Connor shifted his position on the bed of pine needles he was sitting on. He glanced over at his partner as she sat staring at the sea.

"You see, Anna, this cruising life is boring," he expostulated to his grinning mate. "Nothing to do sitting on a sail boat all day, right?"

Tom recalled the passage they had made rail down in a force eight gale in breaking seas, close reaching off Cape Hatteras, hell bound for Florida or bust, having been at sea for three days and as many nights.

"Drive you nuts being out here bored to death, eh?"

Anna O'Connor, in her husband's imagination, looked as exhausted as he remembered being himself during that tough passage south.

"Yes, Tom," she seemed to be saying again with a whimsical smile, "I'm bored stiff."

Tom O'Connor's mind ranged through the past, sampling memories of experiences ashore that he and Anna had shared. He recalled the dingy port town diner where they had expected little, but were surprised by a four-star banquet. He remembered the hike they had made for buffalo steaks three miles out of town to a place called Grandview Farms, where the view of the surrounding sea and the harbor were not grand, but magnificent. The buffalo steaks too were not grand, but magnificent. Making love and the evening stroll along the pier were not grand, but also magnificent.

The memories emerged as a collage of images. O'Connor recalled the boats, the fine boats of Newfoundland, Southampton, Portland, Dublin, Saint Thomas, and Lunenberg, Nova Scotia and the port towns and harbors of picturesque beauty. He relived the terror of the storms. They had been through great storms off Canso Head, off Yarmouth, and Hatteras. Passing Cape Cod, they had taken the outside passage and came to fear for their lives when lightning hissed in the water and Saint Elmo's fire danced in the rigging for the first and only time during their years at sea. But Tom O'Connor's most precious memories ashore were of love, her love for him, his love for her.

Until death do us part.

Tom O'Connor sought solace from the pain of his inconsolable loss in memories of those special times he and his co-skipper had shared, times when cruising under sail had become crazy, zenned out, and unreal. Those were the times when he and Anna had heard the sound of one hand clapping.

Such experiences had not happened often enough and they had turned up unexpectedly. Maybe on a hot summer day with *Annie* reaching in a ten knot breeze making four or five knots and the harbor she is approaching sits like a picture postcard just under the foot of her headsail. That harbor grows larger ever so slowly. Gradually, time stops and the sailor in grace with the sea leans into the cockpit bulkhead, holding hands with a precious mate and anticipating a good swim. The sailor sits quietly with his mate as the ship falls softly and sweetly into the swells and the harbor looms closer. Everything that matters in the world lies contained within the frame of his vision as he savors the loving embrace that is evolving between his ship and that no longer distant harbor. The vibrant distortions of heat in the air tease the fibers of the mind apart, freeing it from the constraints of rationality. Finally, the reality behind the appearances of things washes over the sailor in grace with the sea like a gently breaking wave and it does not matter if that ship or those sailors ever reach that harbor. Maybe they are still out there sailing somewhere together again.

Tom O'Connor can see *Annie* in a landlocked anchorage riding at anchor upon a sheet of forest green glass surrounded by boulders, pink and gray granite sentinels, festooned by birch trees and sycamores. Tom and Anna are sitting in the cockpit at sunset, not speaking but listening to a sylvan symphony as the bird song grows in intensity. The fervor of avian communication then begins to slowly diminish as dusk comes on. Gulls are fishing nearby. The ripples from a breaking tail fin are approaching the ship in a movement that seems to parallel the expansion of the universe. Heavy lidded and serene, Tom O'Connor can feel his skin absorbing the spirit of this place as he sits seemingly suspended in midair, not rooted to anything.

Then the sky begins to fade and the rocks begin to crumble and the trees become as tall and graceful beneath the still water as above it. At last, there is no above or below as the ripples edge closer and the musicians in the bird symphony begin to take encores as distinct and individual voices. The dusk grows deeper, the first star appears, and the bird cries continue to die away, each statement less frequent, less intense, and less real.

Tom O'Connor can sense his and Anna's place in this scene. He can sense the dissolution of the diaphanous, no longer limiting boundaries of her skin. He can feel himself penetrating her space and she his. He feels less two beings than one, savoring this exquisite moment until the next time they can live it together again in some other place.

Tom O'Connor rose to his feet, relishing the bittersweet afterglow of this treasured memory. He could never live such a scene again in any other place. He felt like the he-bird in Walt Whitman's poem, searching for its mate along Paumanok's shore. That terrible word *death*, not low and delicious, was still out of the cradle endlessly rocking.

"No," Tom said softly. The story was not supposed to have ended the way it had.

He began to make his way back down the trail that led to Camden. He felt heavy and torpid, but he pushed his body headlong down the steep incline.

The years had passed quickly for Anna and Tom. They had made a couple of grand circuits down the Atlantic coast, from Nova Scotia to the Dry Tortugas. Then, when Tom O'Connor was fifty-three and Claire was twenty-one, Rachel had been born.

Claire had never married. When questioned about Rachel's father, her only response had been elusive.

"Don't talk to me about conventional life styles, you two of all people!" Tongue in cheek, she had added, "Not to worry though. He is of good breeding stock. He is intelligent and artistic, but not the kind of person you would want for a son-in-law!"

And so, Rachel O'Connor had been born into an unconventional family during unconventional times. Tom O'Connor recalled that magical day in the birthing room when he had, with trepidation, received into his hands a tiny being in the first moments of her life. She had seemed not at all keen to be among the born, emitting with all of her strength a lusty cry of protest as she struggled to get a small fist into her mouth. Tom recalled the sense of wonder he had experienced at that moment of instant heart lock. The emotion had contained a sense of mortality, a sense of the futility of pressing too hard against the slow march of time. The melancholy of the moment had been tempered by wonder and by instantaneous love for a tiny being on loan, whose life he knew he would probably never follow to completion.

Some grandfather he had become, he berated himself soberly. The birth of their granddaughter had presented Tom and Anna with a classic dilemma. They had debated the issues with deliberation. Should they give up the boat, stay close, become doting grandparents, or go ahead with their cruising plans? The decision to go on had been mutual, but bittersweet. The rocking chairs were put temporarily on hold.

With bitterness and guilt, Tom thought of his role as Rachel's grandfather. All he could show for himself was a sad legacy of Christmas and birthday presents, phone calls and letters. He castigated himself for the absence of substance in any of these things.

Tom and Anna O'Connor had sailed the *Anna Livia* across the Atlantic Ocean to Ireland. Tom had been reading the works of James

Joyce for years. The landfall in Ireland and subsequent visit to Dublin afforded him an opportunity to make his pilgrimage to Joyce Country. *Annie's* formal name had been culled from *Finnegans Wake.*

The O'Connors had cruised the Irish coast to Galway and the Aran Islands, then up to the Skerries, and then around the North shore to Dublin. With *Annie* moored at Dun Leary Marina south of Dublin, Tom and Anna had spent the ensuing winter traipsing through the streets of the Irish capital, seeking what was left of the Joycean haunts.

In the spring, the O'Connors had made the passage across the Irish Sea to England and Scotland, spending another winter in Great Britain before reaching the continent the following year. The time he and Anna had spent cruising the canals and rivers of France and Germany, or ranging the ancient Mediterranean ports had left Tom O'Connor with a collage of memories, the individual threads of experience now woven into a vast tapestry.

Like all of life's grand experiences, the O'Connors' six-year European odyssey had seemed to end only too quickly. Following the northeast trade winds, they had piloted *Annie* back across the Atlantic to Barbados in the Caribbean. Both transatlantic passages had proven anticlimactic. The O'Connors had encountered no big storms, no prolonged calms, icebergs, submarines, amorous whale, or floating obstructions. *Annie* had surged along on both passages in remarkably steady following winds and quartering seas. Her wake at night aglow with soft green phosphorescence, *Annie* had sailed on, happy and free like Anna and Tom.

Nothing so wonderful should ever have to end, Tom protested with bitterness, as he crashed down the trail to Camden. But end it had in a little cabaret in Barbados. Anna and Tom had been celebrating the success of the passage. They were toasting Poseidon, Aeolus, Thetis, and all of the sea nymphs when Anna had placed her head in her hands complaining of a headache. Anna O'Connor had long been subject to post stress migraines, so neither of them had been all that concerned at first. Before there had been time to think about any kind of remedy, however, Anna had collapsed in Tom's arms. He could not have known at the time how bad this was going to be.

The gracious, empathetic maitre d' had summoned an ambulance, but Anna O'Connor had lost consciousness by then. Numb with shock and disbelief, Tom had listened to the strange foreign sound of the siren. The whine was like the bleating terror of some dying animal. Tom could not possibly have known that his own existence was never to be the same from that horrifying moment on. He had cradled his dying wife in his arms, unable to take his eyes from the terrible distortions that had disfigured her familiar, still beautiful face. Tom sat watching in that face, the slow dissolution of over forty years of love.

The house physician at the hospital had been understanding and patient with Tom. He had explained his diagnosis of intra-cranial hemorrhage and he had commiserated over the dismal prognosis. Undoubtedly, he had faced the helpless irrationality of foreigners in times of such incapacitating stress many times. He had acceded to Tom O'Connor's demand that air evacuation of his wife to the United States be attempted. He had even made a few preliminary calls.

Dr. Mirbeau had been kind and reassuring, but not condescending in any way. Tom O'Connor would come to respect and admire him for that later. At the time, however, Tom had only been able to feel an emotion so strange and so terrible in reference to this kind man that his feelings had been beyond categorization. This twisted, wrenching feeling had come when Dr. Mirbeau had placed his hand on Tom's shoulder in the hospital waiting room that day.

"I am sorry, Monsieur O'Connor," he had said, his eyes sad and careworn, "but your wife is dead."

Tom had staggered from the hospital. He may have walked the streets for hours or even days. He may have become senselessly drunk. No events had been recorded on the blank pages of his consciousness until he had become aware some time later of the strange fact that someone *had* arranged for the air evacuation of his wife to the United States. He had found himself sitting in an airplane moving rapidly through space, traveling with Anna, but she was no longer with him. He had not been able to bear the thought of her alone, exiled to some barren place within the bowels of the aircraft. He had not been able to bear the thought of her at all.

Chapter Seven

After reaching town, Tom ambled along Camden's main street for some time before he finally walked into the *Mariner's Restaurant*, a red shingled building with candy striped awnings on Route One. He tried to anchor himself to the present, but the past would not yet release him. He ordered an expresso, his and Anna's favorite mid-afternoon drink, but the waitress informed him that the *Mariner's* does not serve expresso.

With some irritation, Tom ordered regular coffee and then took a seat in one of the booths. The waitress eyed him with suspicion, since one of the bar stools at the counter might have been more appropriate for a single patron. She was also concerned because Tom seemed to be offering sugar to a person with whom he was conducting a fragmented monologue.

"The funeral was beautiful, Anna," he said, as if she had not been there herself. He described the details once again.

"Claire arranged to have them play all of the old songs you loved," he assured his ghost.

"Yes, the funeral had been beautiful," Tom's ghost admitted.

Following Anna O'Connor's death, Claire and Rachel had urged Tom to stay with them.

"You can have my room, Tom," Rachel had suggested. O'Connor had encouraged his granddaughter to address him by his given name, to the great consternation of Claire and Anna. But her grandfather had not been able to accept Rachel's proposal. *Annie*, lying in a marina in Barbados, was drawing him back to her.

"I wanted to stay with Claire and Rachel," Tom blurted aloud. "I thought maybe I'd sell the boat, but I just couldn't let her go, Anna. You understand that I couldn't do that, don't you?" he implored. The waitress fidgeted and kept a close eye on her peculiar patron.

Anna O'Connor was dressed in an old oiled wool sweater, sipping sugary sweet expresso in the booth with her husband. Of course she understood. Anna always understood.

Tom O'Connor had returned to Barbados within a month of his wife's funeral. Despite the security arrangements the American Consulate had arranged through the marina operator—an Englishman named Henchly—thieves had broken into the *Anna Livia* and had violated her, ripping out her companion way doors with a crowbar. She had been stripped of her navigation instruments. Several items of great personal value—*Annie's* trawler lamp, a porcelain angel, and a set of copper cookware—had also been taken. The *Cassens & Plath* sextant that had guided the O'Connors across the Atlantic and a mahogany and glass encased barograph were both missing. The thieves, apparently lacking either sophistication or culture, had passed over Anna's valuable print of Rogier van der Weyden's *Portrait of a Lady*.

Once the shock of the devastation inflicted on his boat had subsided, Tom had rushed to a forepeak locker where he found—to his relief—his wife's musical jewelry box, which had been stowed among the lifejackets to protect it during the passage from Grand Canaria to Barbados. Tom removed the plastic wrapping from the box. As he opened its lid, the familiar refrain of Pachelbel's *Canon in D* wafted into the air, bringing with it a flood of painful, but treasured memories. He extracted and fingered in turn the bracelets, earrings, lockets, and necklaces that had belonged to his wife.

Later that afternoon, Tom had stormed into Henchly's office. The fat Brit sat sweating in the tropical heat behind his filthy desk. Tom was livid. His anger with Henchly stemmed from his sense of injustice and grief, together with his conviction that the manager was guilty of complicity in *Annie's* defacement and pilfering.

Tom had walked over to Henchly, wrenched his head back and shoved the barrel of a twelve-gauge flare gun into manager's mouth. Henchly had managed a garbled protest as Tom stood over him debating whether to pull the trigger. When Tom had eventually backed off, Henchly's stream of dockyard profanity and vituperation had followed O'Connor all the way back to *Annie.* Henchly's guilt seemed established, however, when he made no effort to evict Tom during the month and a half of labor required for the restoration of the *Anna Livia.* Tom helped himself to the tools and the materials he needed from the marina workshop without protest from Henchly.

"What?" Tom O'Connor shouted with a start. The waitress had gently touched his arm.

"Sir, please," she cautioned, "the other patrons!"

Henchly's betrayal and near murder had become part of the public domain. Tom peered at the perplexed faces that were starring fixedly at him.

"I should have killed that fat bastard!" he explained to his captive audience. Placing a hefty tip into the cold, damp hand of the young waitress, Tom picked up his past and left the *Mariner's,* after offering the unsolicited opinion that several of the nautical artifacts that adorned the walls were considerably gaudy and overdone.

During the time he had spent in Barbados, Tom O'Connor had torn out every square inch of wood on the *Anna Livia* that had been mutilated by the thieves or damaged by the weather. He had located a local woodworker who had been able to craft a new set of companionway doors. Tom had worked dawn to dusk sanding, staining, varnishing, and waxing each new piece of wood until *Annie's* interior had been restored to near perfect condition. He had stripped and oiled her teak and he had polished all of her brass and chrome.

When he had replaced *Annie's* navigation instruments and repurchased exact duplications of as many of the stolen personal items as he was able to buy through special orders from the United States, Tom finally left the marina in Barbados. No doubt, Henchly had been relieved to see him go.

On the day Tom O'Connor had taken her through the outer breakwater into the open sea under full sail, the *Anna Livia*, Whiskey, Tango, X-ray 2773 had been restored to near perfect condition.

There followed a series of dark nights of the soul for Tom O'Connor. For several months his life became a tormented hell. Drunk most of the time on *Montego Bay* rum, he pushed *Annie* up the chain of the Antilles Islands, sailing with reckless abandon, riding most of the time on the fringes of disaster.

Tom had experienced an ominous and lonely ocean whose ebb and flow ranges between deadly silence, the roar of the wind, and the mournful imagined cries of sea hags. The ocean he sailed was torn and tormented, a sea which spews its wrecks upon its endless shore and howls like a ravished banshee for more victims to feed on.

Tom O'Connor came to understand and respect the terrible isolation of the single-handed sailor, as he assumed the role himself. He and Anna had observed these wraith-like souls in many of the ports and anchorages they had visited. Tom had responded in the past to these solitary sailors—with no justification—with pity and not a little fear. He had never been able to imagine them happy, though some of them doubtlessly were so. Now as a single-handler himself, episodes of loneliness had borne down on him like an incubus. During those early months following Anna's death, he found his only consolation in alcohol.

Ashore, he became a frenzied animal haunting the market squares in the Carib island port towns, drawn and wasted in body and spirit. He drowned his pain in sickly booze, spending hours in the innumerable island bars that seem to be there to meet just such primitive needs. At sea, he pushed *Annie* to the limits, keeping her over sailed and straining to weather in all conditions, drunk and sick most of the time on rum or the effects of the rolling ocean.

Tom had considered every form of more direct and efficient suicide, but he was unable to bring himself to make an end to his life. He was chagrined to find he did not have the awesome strength of the true suicide. Still, he pushed the sea close to its limits, recalling Synge's quotation of the Aran islanders: "A man who is not afraid of the sea will soon be drownded, for he will be going out on a day he shouldn't. But we do be afraid of the sea and we do only be drownded now and again."

Tom O'Connor had lost his fear of the sea. He went out on many days when he should not have. He was always amazed when he made the next port and found he had not been "drownded".

By the end of that first summer following his wife's death, Tom O'Connor reached the U.S. mainland. Unexpectedly, he found something about his return to places he and Anna had visited together strangely reviving. As he walked streets they had walked or ate in restaurants they had frequented, he began to sense her presence in his life again. He began to feel that she was with him once more.

Then, on his sixty-first birthday, Tom impulsively dragged himself into an empty Catholic Church in a port town near Saint Augustine. In that quiet place, he had fallen to his knees and had emptied himself in an outpouring of grief and pain and had asked to be helped. At that moment, something strange happened. A form, that of a woman, but with her face masked with a dark veil, entered the building and proceeded through the Stations of the Cross, encircling Tom O'Connor as he knelt in one of the central pews.

Tom never gave much thought to the many rational explanations that might have accounted for this event. He had needed a sign of some kind and this was to be his sign of grace. He had never before witnessed such an occurrence in any of the many Catholic churches he had been in. For Tom, that dark form had been an angel.

Tom O'Connor and his wife had collected representations of angels. Anna had thought of them as beings with the answers to those perplexing questions about life which torment the human spirit. Tom thought of angels more prosaically as messengers. He felt that a message had been delivered to him in that church outside Saint Augustine. What the message was exactly, he didn't yet know. He concluded that he was being told to go on with his life. Perhaps his angel was telling him he would be needed again some day.

Tom began reading the liturgical offices at this point, picking up an outdated set of *The Liturgy of the Hours* in bookstore in that same town. He cut back drastically on his use of alcohol. He then began to make his circuits of the Atlantic coast, sailing *Annie* north or south with the seasons from the Florida Keys to Cape Breton, Nova Scotia. Shortly after this, Anna O'Connor, a ghost of her husband's imagination, had returned to share his life once more at sea.

Chapter Eight

The Camden Post Office on Chestnut Street resembles a bank more than a dispensary of stamps and a depository of letters. Entering the brownish brick building, Tom dropped the letter he had written that morning to his daughter, Claire, into the out of town slot. He then approached the counter and handed the clerk his MCCA card.

"Anything for me in general delivery?" he asked. Expecting another day of waiting, he was pleasantly surprised when he was handed a manila envelope bearing his name.

Tom carried the package outside and then ambled over to the park that terraces Camden's inner harbor. He sat down on one of the benches to examine his mail. His financial statements were there, as were two editions of *Cruising World* magazine and a copy of the *James Joyce Quarterly*.

Tom tucked the letter written in his daughter's familiar hand into the breast pocket of his shirt for reading later. His more immediate attention had been piqued by the unexpected. There was an official looking letter addressed to him from the Michigan State Department of Social Services. Claire and Rachel lived in Michigan. Tom tore open the letter and read it.

"Dear Mr. O'Connor,

It is imperative that you contact me at once. I have been trying to reach you through the United States Coast Guard, but without success. If this letter reaches you, phone me day or night at the following numbers."

The letter was signed, Sheila Ingrahm, MSW. Home and office telephone numbers were listed.

Years before, Tom and Anna O'Connor had agreed to monitor the emergency frequencies on VHF and single side band radio every day from 1200-1300 EST for urgent messages. As he read over Ms Ingrahm's letter, Tom realized he had been lax in monitoring calls in recent months. It was understandable that the Coast Guard had been unable to establish contact with the *Anna Livia*.

The letter was obviously disturbing. Tom called Ms Ingrahm's business number at once, only to be informed that she was out sick. He decided to call her at home.

A heady, congested voice answered the phone, but perked up at once as soon as he had identified himself.

"Thank God you've called me, Mr. O'Connor."

"Bad news, I take it?" he tentatively suggested.

"Well," Ms Ingrahm hesitated, "I don't quite know how to put this, Mr. O'Connor. Over the phone, I mean."

So it was to be more bad news.

"I've taken a few knocks in the past, Ms Ingrahm," Tom said with resignation. "Why don't you just do what you have to do."

Tom O'Connor's daughter, Claire, had been killed in an automobile accident seventeen days earlier. There were sketchy details—a rain-slicked road, maybe a drunk—but not much of it registered. Tom hung on as the sympathetic words emerged from the other end of the receiver. The wrenching impact of the message impaled him to the phone. Rachel was a temporary ward of the State of Michigan. There was to be a custody hearing and the possible placement of Tom's granddaughter into a foster home. The funeral arrangements had been handled by one of Claire's friends.

"I'm so sorry, Mr. O'Connor," Ms Ingrahm said. Then, realizing that he had not yet spoken a word, she added with alarm, "Are you all right, Mr. O'Connor?"

"Am I all right, Anna? Am I all right?" Tom whispered inaudibly.

Finally able to respond, Tom managed to copy the necessary addresses and phone numbers onto the back of the envelope. He would be meeting Ms Ingrahm in her office in 48 hours. He placed a call to his granddaughter, but the conversation was strained. Tom told Rachel that he was coming to see her, but the voice on the other end of the line, sounding mature beyond his granddaughter's eleven years, was non-committal. Tom realized he could have expected little more.

He stumbled away from the telephone. Reaching the bench he had previously occupied, he extracted the letter from his breast pocket.

"Dear Daddy," it read, "I hope this finds you well. Rachel and I enjoyed your call last month. We were glad to hear things are stable. We have no intriguing news from our end. Rachel grows. She's becoming a gangly, pre-adolescent, gawky little kid. Can you believe she'll be twelve on her next birthday? I grow every day, thanks to you and Momma. Did you know I had a happy childhood? I know why you stay with the boat, Daddy. I really do. But just remember, sea rover, there's always a place for you on land. Anytime! Oh, I met a new one since I spoke with you last. Mike-all! I'll tell you all about him next time, unless he fades away like all the rest. Love you, Claire."

Tom read the letter over again word for word, then syllable by syllable. He thought of the inane words he had penned to his daughter that morning. His own letter was destined to reach someone detached and remote from Claire or himself. How would such a person assess the relationship he had had with his daughter? Not well.

Mustering his strength, Tom returned to the Chestnut Street Post Office and concocted a story about having forgotten to put the most important item in the letter, the check. The unsuspecting clerk retrieved the envelope. Tom's letter to his daughter would remain unopened and obviously unread, stuck between the pages of one of his books.

Leaving the post office, Tom found his dinghy and rowed out the only sanctuary available to him, to *Annie.* He paced her decks, explaining things in wild gesticulations to his wife. Yes, she too had heard the shocking news. From *Annie's* bowsprit, Tom stood looking up into the darkening sky over the Camden hills. Lowering clouds signaled the approach of a rapidly advancing depression.

As he tried to comprehend this unexpected turn of events, Tom O'Connor's sense of his abject failure as a parent and grandparent seemed to be rolling through his mind like the clouds scudding in from the turbulent horizon. Where had he ever been when he was really needed? He thought of Claire, hoping her end had been swift and painless. He could not bear the possibility that she had suffered. He thought of Rachel, bereft of any support from him during her time of greatest need. Tom O'Connor's life seemed an empty sham, a vacuous indulgence in self-pity.

Tom tore the covers from *Annie's* sails. He felt an overwhelming need to take her out to sea. The falling pressure registered by the barograph in the saloon was unheeded, as Tom clanged away at the windlass. Once *Annie* was free of the bottom, he hauled her main halyard, raising a full mainsail with reckless impatience.

The wind had risen to a screaming force six as *Annie* reached the Graves. A more prudent yachtsman, making port in time, hailed an unheeded warning, but Tom recklessly made for the open ocean. Death seemed to have assumed control of every aspect of his wretched existence.

The wind came onto the sea as a tremendous downdraft. The sky darkened to an eerie green. The first heavy gust swept out of the scud roll with a whine that made the rigging shudder. The fury of the oncoming wind knocked the belabored ship down onto her beam-ends into the blackening, churning water. *Annie* recovered momentarily, but moaned with the stresses of too much canvas for the quickening storm.

She pulled to weather, her helm submitting to the relentless wind, but Tom in his madness held her bow off the gusts. The shrieking wind battered *Annie* back onto her beam-ends, sending her floundering out of control, her mast nearly touching the building waves.

A bolt of lightning shattered the surface of the sea not five hundred yards off. In the momentary light, Tom could see white horses riding the seas like the *Four Horsemen of the Apocalypse*, but all of the riders were *Death.* Death seemed to be everywhere in those threatening seas, in the thunder, in the wind, and in the rain. What matter if his demise and *Annie's* were added to such a disheartening compendium of death?

Annie shuddered and then fell with a resounding crash into the trough of a massive rogue wave. Lying on her beam, broaching and helpless with green water pouring into her cockpit, she seemed to be crying in her rigging for relief, but Tom—maddened now with grief, anguish, and self-castigation—would not relent. His eyes were afire from the needle points of the slashing rain, but he could still see death raging through the building seas.

"Let it end now," he said aloud, "let it all end here and now."

"Heave to and reef!"

The forceful command had come to him out of the fury of the storm. He peered into the darkness. Anna was sitting in the cockpit in harness, the carbine hook of her lanyard clipped to *Annie's* safety line. She called out to Tom again.

"Heave to and reef!"

"Why, Anna?" he cried to his insistent ghost, a cry resounding with futility and self-loathing. "It's no good. It's no good anymore."

He could hardly make out his wife's familiar form in the cockpit less than four feet away. A torrent of rain was pelting his skin. *Annie*, rail down and struggling to weather, was slicing through the now monstrous seas. Thunder was rumbling through the sky and through Tom O'Connor's heaving heart.

"Why reef?" he cried out, his voice ringing with bitter resignation.

He could not make out what Anna was saying at first. He strained into the darkness, into the vacuum in which she sat and from where she spoke. Her words finally bridged the chasm between his grief-stricken brain and sense.

"Because of Rachel," she said, her voice ringing with unassailable finality.

Part II

Rachel

Chapter One

Wayfarer Marine had a transient slip available when Tom O'Connor radioed a request the morning following the storm. He had spent a sleepless night at sea hove to until the severe weather had abated. He had made harbor with the rising sun. Tom managed a couple of hours of sleep, then he battened *Annie* down and hiked out Union Street to the *U-Save Auto Rental* at *Smith's Garage* in Rockport. By noon, he was on his way to Michigan.

Tom would not fly, not since the flight back from Barbados.

As the miles passed, the memory of his daughter eased in and out of his consciousness like a quiet sea bathing a rock awash. He could not believe that Claire too was now lost to him.

Tom tried to recall as much as he could about custody law, digging into his professional past, but he had not practiced that specialty and he had no idea what the Michigan statues might be. Besides, as far as Rachel was concerned, he had weighed his options and had all ready made his decision. Anna O'Connor, as was always the case, agreed with Tom's plan.

Tom contemplated the impression he would probably make at a custody hearing. He caught a glimpse of himself in the rear view mirror, craning his neck and pushing his hair back so he could anticipate the effect of his earring. He smiled at his own scraggly face and then at Anna, before breaking into a cackling and nearly hysterical fit of laughter.

"Can't you just hear the judge," he chuckled, poking Anna gently in the ribs, "This guy is supposed to be a lawyer! My brother at the bar of law!"

Tom O'Connor was not going to attend the custody hearing concerning his granddaughter.

"Fat chance they'd give her to us anyway," he said soberly.

Tom had made his decision about Rachel.

Chapter Two

An unmistakable mingling of surprise and disappointment was immediately apparent on the face of Sheila Ingrahm, as Tom O'Connor was ushered into her office at the State Department of Social Services building near Ann Arbor, Michigan.

Ms. Ingrahm's demeanor was pleasant, but soberly professional. She looked driven, probably a typical workaholic, Tom surmised. He was sure she had probably expected a distinguished looking retired lawyer of independent means with immaculate nails and a head of closely cropped gray hair.

Tom realized he did not look his best. He had tied his hair in a ponytail, but he had not slept much in three nights. His eyes were puffy and had deep circles beneath them, which probably made him appear chronically ill.

Ms. Ingrahm assumed the deportment appropriate to her role as Rachel's advocate.

"Your granddaughter, Mr. O'Connor, has been made a temporary ward of the state, as I informed you when we discussed her situation over the phone," Ms. Ingrahm explained. "Judge Martin felt that was the only proper course of action to take while I pursued my efforts to locate you. You know, of course, that you are Rachel's only surviving relative."

Ms. Ingrahm paused. Tom realized she was monitoring his reactions. She may have had some doubt about his ability to comprehend the situation. He liked her immensely.

"I understand," he said with a nod.

"Now that I have located you, the hearing concerning Rachel's custody can proceed. Given the circumstances, I believe we could get the judge to schedule that on a fast track," Ms. Ingrahm continued.

Tom glanced in Anna's direction, but checked the comment he was going to make. He sat massaging his beard with a look on his face that Sheila Ingrahm charitably interpreted as distant.

"You would have to make a formal request for custody, Mr. O'Connor, but quite frankly, I don't..."

Sheila Ingrahm hesitated. She seemed to have noticed Tom's earring for the first time.

"The child custody judge in this case has responsibility for Rachel's welfare, Mr. O'Connor. You would have to convince the magistrate that the child would have a proper home and that she would receive acceptable guidance and education."

Ms. Ingrahm was obviously trying to be gentle. She seemed to have forgotten for the moment that Tom had once practiced law.

"Grandparents are often awarded custody of their orphaned grandchildren, Mr. O'Connor," Ms Ingrahm said. Then she removed her glasses and placed them on her desk.

"Let me be perfectly frank with you, Mr. O'Connor. Can I do that?"

Tom nodded.

"Even if you were to clean up your act, let us say. Trim your beard, get a haircut, get rid of that little item of jewelry you have in your ear, I think the judge would have serious reservations about awarding custody to you because of your lifestyle."

Ms. Ingrahm's expression was apologetic, but committed. She continued.

"I think there would probably be fatal concerns by any responsible magistrate about a person trying to raise his granddaughter aboard this sailboat you live on. I do realize that on board education through correspondence schools is accomplished successfully on rare occasions by particularly stable families. Would you consider taking up residence ashore, in a conventional home?"

This last question was far too absurd to merit a response.

"You shouldn't judge a book by its cover," he said, giving Anna a sidelong glance.

"I beg your pardon?" Ms. Ingrahm asked.

"I don't want custody," Tom said flatly.

Perhaps Sheila Ingrahm had seen enough of a cynical society to be able to contain any surprise Tom's last remark may have engendered.

"I see," she said without emotion.

"I mean, I agree with you," Tom said emphatically, "a sailboat is no place to raise a child, especially a girl. I just came out here to visit Rachel for a few hours and to John Hancock any papers you might need me to sign."

The chauvinism in Tom's remark was not the only thing Sheila Ingrahm winced at. She folded Rachel's file and neatly placed it to the side.

"You know," he said, mustering as much warmth as he was able, "I'd like to take Rachel out to dinner, to a spot somewhere nearby. We could have a nice evening together, the two of us. That would be possible, wouldn't it? I mean, I am her grandfather."

Tom tried to dissect the complex expression on Sheila Ingrahm's face. The dominant element was clearly a mixture of incredulity and disdain, but there was more. There was sadness and a great deal of empathy. Yes, he liked her very much.

"The visitation will have to be chaperoned," Ms Ingrahm pronounced in a tone that left no possibility of equivocation.

This was a wrinkle, one Tom had not anticipated. He was taken aback, but immediately regained composure.

"We would be delighted to have you aboard," he lied, summoning bonhomie. "Do you drink red wine or white, my dear Ms. Ingrahm?"

"I am afraid that chaperoning is not in my job description, Mr. O'Connor. You will have to take Rachel to a family style restaurant that does not serve alcohol and your chaperone will be one of the nuns."

"One of the nuns," Tom parroted with surprise. "You mean one of the nuns from the home?"

Tom knew that his granddaughter was living in a home operated by the *Sisters of the Immaculate Heart of Mary*, but he had been unaware that chaperoning family outings was part of a nun's job description either.

"Yes, one of the nuns," Ms Ingrahm said dryly.

Tom could appreciate that the interview was becoming burdensome for Rachel's social worker.

"Well, one of the nuns it is then!" he said, making a quick sign of the cross. "Dominoes and biscuits, and all the rest."

Chapter Three

Sheila Ingrahm had insisted upon an ironclad verbal contract with Tom O'Connor concerning the restrictions the State of Michigan felt obligated to impose upon his single night on the town with Rachel. He was to pick up his granddaughter and the chaperone at the convent at 4:30 P.M.—1630 in a sailor's lingo.

Tom spent a restless afternoon killing time until the hour appointed for his visit. He had not intended to do so, but found himself compelled to visit the memorial gardens where Claire's ashes had been interred. They found the site, he and Anna, in a mausoleum centered within a grove of pines. Tom wondered whether Claire would have been pleased with the location, idyllic as some kind soul had tried to make it. The thought of ashes frightened Tom. He recalled a scattering of ashes, a scattering of ashes at sea. He repressed the memory immediately.

He and Claire had never discussed "last wishes." As for himself, Tom was hoping the sharks or the sea birds would get him in the end or that some fellow sailor would find him mummified by the sun, sitting rigidly at *Annie's* helm somewhere adrift far out to sea.

He and Anna sat for hours in the shade of the pine grove surrounding the mausoleum, rehashing the details of Tom's decision about Rachel. The decision was pragmatic, something that just had to be done.

For the remainder of the afternoon Tom drove about aimlessly. He made a few purchases and then—with a sailor's instinct—ferreted out the waterfront in nearby Detroit. He watched boats for about an hour or two and then he popped into the *Old Mariners' Church* on Jefferson Avenue, where he sat in a pew trying to remember the lyrics to Gordon Lightfoot's ballad about the *Edmund Fitzgerald*. He was anxious to get back to *Annie* and the sea.

The convent of the *Sisters of the Immaculate Heart of Mary* was located on a four or five acre tract of land several miles outside of Ann Arbor, where Claire and Rachel had lived. The convent house was a Gothic revival jewel in masonry, with flying buttresses that didn't actually fly, but with enough stained glass and pointed arches to capture an effect. Tom O'Connor could easily imagine living a contemplative life in such a place.

Early for his appointment, he ambled over the grounds. He was unable to make direct eye contact with the wimpled figures that knelt or sat within pleasant niches nestled among the trees. He could sense the vague presence of spirits, perhaps the spirits of dead nuns, flittering like butterflies among the lilac bushes and flower beds. He was surprised that none of the orphans or wards of the court were in sight.

The Mother Superior who greeted Tom in the convent house was curt and explicit in her instructions. The restaurant would have to be suitable. She made several suggestions. Rachel and Sister Emilia, the escort, would have to be back in time for prayers at compline, before 9:00 P.M.—2100 in a sailor's lingo.

After his orientation and briefing, Tom was left alone while Rachel and Sister Emilia were summoned. The reception room was a museum of religious icons and artifacts. Tom wandered among the triptychs, illuminated books of the hours, reliquaries, and monstrances until his name was called.

Sister Emilia discreetly moved off to a nook in one corner of the room. From this perspective, she carefully monitored the interchange between Rachel and her grandfather. Tom noticed at once that Sister Emilia was not in habit, but was dressed in "civilian" clothes. Her demeanor left him with the impression that she might have been willing to exchange any penance for her present assignment.

Rachel stood just inside the doorway. She had grown since the previous Thanksgiving, when Tom had seen her last. She was the gangly preteen Claire had described in her letter, but her usual exuberance was not in evidence. Her face was that of a young girl in mourning.

Tom embraced Rachel, but found her stiff and unyielding. He planted a kiss on her cheek.

"Well, you're looking well," he lied.

The moment was awkward. Tom could feel Sister Emilia watching him intently. No doubt she had been made aware that Mr. O'Connor was the grandfather who was abandoning his granddaughter. Heaven only knew what Rachel had been told.

"Why don't we get some dinner," Tom suggested feebly. Sister Emilia and Rachel moved woodenly toward the door. Tom was convinced that both of his guests were anxious to get this over as soon as possible. Other than a weak greeting from Rachel, neither she nor Sister Emilia had spoken a word.

Tom fumbled through a trial of small talk as the trio walked stiffly to his rented car. He could elicit nothing but monosyllables in response. The situation had all of the markings of an extremely long night.

Once the group was ensconced in the car, Tom turned to Sister Emilia.

"Now, I've always been a reasonably good Catholic, Sister E, so I'm going to ask you to cooperate with me here, as one fellow pilgrim to another."

"What do you mean by cooperation, Mr. O'Connor?" Sister Emilia asked.

"Well, I'd like to have a nice outing with my granddaughter and with you, of course. Life is short, you know. So, I'm going to ask you to skip the family diner and let me pick out a nice place where I can get a small glass of wine. If you want to stretch the rules and take a nip yourself, I swear I'll never tell a soul."

Addressing Rachel, Tom prodded his granddaughter.

"You wouldn't rat on the good Sister, would you?"

"No," Rachel said flatly, with a pained expression on her face.

"Good, then that settles it," Tom concluded with relief. "I'll pick the spot."

Thomas O'Connor did not pick the spot, of course. Sister Emilia's calm restatement of the rules proved to be an instant replay of the Mother Superior's earlier injunctions. Tom was left in awe of the vow of obedience. At least he had not been subjected to a discourse on the evils of drink.

Once he, Rachel, and Sister Emilia had been seated amid a bevy of screaming kids and exasperated parents in the first acceptable family style restaurant the three had encountered, Tom ordered a large pitcher of ice water, coffee for himself, and a soda for Rachel. Sister Emilia was persuaded to accept a cup of tea.

"Sure has been warm, hasn't it?" Tom suggested, as he refilled Sister Emilia's glass with ice water at every opportunity.

Tom carried on a running monologue—since neither of his guests had much to say—about *Annie*. He was careful not to mention her present port of call.

The group had started a second pitcher of ice water and their salads had been served, when a slightly discomfited Sister Emilia announced her intention to visit the ladies' room. Tom offered a silent prayer at this pronouncement, having speculated about possible methods of penance employed by nuns in public places.

Unfortunately, Rachel chimed in, "I'm going too, Tom."

"Rachel, Rachel" Tom expostulated, placing a hand firmly on his granddaughter's arm. "Hold on there just a minute."

Tom turned imploringly to Sister Emilia, who had risen from her chair. He gave the young nun his best rendition of grandfatherly anguish.

"I haven't had a single minute to talk to you alone," Tom whined. "I want to tell you about your new trust fund."

To his great relief, Sister Emilia demurely withdrew in the direction of the heads.

Tom immediately sprung into action. He pulled a crinkled envelope from his hip pocket and placed it on Sister Emilia's plate. The envelope contained two fifty-dollar bills and three notes, which Tom had written earlier that afternoon.

The first of these, addressed "T.W.I.M.C.", exonerated Sister Emilia anonymously—since he had not known her name at the time of composition—of any part in a conspiracy. The second was addressed "Dear Sister" and apologized for any embarrassment and suggested a taxi ride back to the convent. Appended to it was a postscript reading: "Pray for us." The final note was addressed to Sheila Ingrahm and simply stated: "Never judge a book by its cover."

Rising from his seat, Tom grabbed his granddaughter by the hand.

"Okay," he said, "let's go. We should be in Maine by dawn."

Perhaps she was shocked into submission by her grandfather's sudden tactic. Perhaps she was only obeying a figure of authority. Maybe there was something about the determination she sensed in Tom's grip on her hand. Maybe Rachel was only responding to deep unexpressed needs of her own. Whatever it was, Rachel O'Connor offered no resistance. She meekly followed her grandfather as he ushered her quickly toward the door.

By 5:30 P.M.—1730 in a sailor's lingo—Rachel and Tom were on the road heading for Camden, Maine, where *Annie* lay waiting. They were miles out of town before the unsuspecting Sister Emilia had reached an empty stall.

Chapter Four

Try as he might, Tom O'Connor was unable to infect his granddaughter with his exuberance over her kidnapping, which seemed to him one of the great crimes of the century. Rachel sat stiffly beside her grandfather, speaking with little spontaneity. Tom's running monologue with the empty space in the back seat contributed to Rachel's reticence.

"Custody hearing be damned, Anna," he cried with a whoop. "We got her out all right, didn't we?"

At the entrance ramp to the eastbound Interstate, Tom eased the car to the shoulder and stopped. He got out and retrieved a large paper bag and a couple of sleeping bags from the trunk. He handed Rachel the sack and then spread the goose down bags on the back seat.

"What was that you ordered at the restaurant," he asked.

Rachel had not yet been tempted to open the bag. She sat holding it on her lap.

"Pork chops," she said hesitantly.

"Yeah, pork chops," Tom echoed wistfully. "Well, I'm sure sorry about those pork chops." He was experiencing regret of his own about the loss of the steak he had ordered.

"Now in that sack you will find a *Big Mac*, a *Whopper*, a *Wendy's* double cheeseburger, a dozen *White Castles*, and a bucket of *Kentucky Fried Chicken*. I couldn't remember which you like best, so I bought them all."

Rachel sat impassively, making no effort to dig into the bag. Tom noticed she was fidgeting some.

"Tom?" she said finally.

"What is it," he asked with disappointment, "you don't like any of those things?"

"I really have to go," she said with unmistakable urgency in her voice.

"Matter of fact, so do I," he said, scanning the road ahead.

"I guess we have a few options," he added. "What will it be, a viaduct, roadside ditch, or the woods?"

"Do you think there might be a rest stop up ahead?" Rachel suggested meekly.

"A rest stop! Listen to this, Anna. She's your granddaughter, all right!"

Tom offered an explanation.

"That's one thing your grandmother will not put up with without a fight. She hates using the woods. Must be a tradition with the women in this family. Was your Momma like that?"

Tom winced. He had promised Anna he would not mention Claire, at least not right away.

Rachel seemed preoccupied with the surrounding terrain. She did not answer his question.

"A rest stop it will be then," Tom said. He was worried that he might have lost some ground after making a reasonably good start.

In addition to providing the necessary relief, the rest stop corrected Tom's oversight about drinks. He bought a jumbo *Coke* for both of them. He watched out of the corner of his eye as Rachel demolished her third piece of *KFC*. At least she had an appetite—a good sign, he concluded.

"What'll you have, Anna?" Tom laughed, with a gesture toward the back seat.

"Your grandmother never lets me eat this junk," he explained to Rachel, flashing her a conspiratorial wink. "Food like this is bad for the cholesterol, but I love it," he added in a whisper as he extracted the greasy contents of a *White Castle* and wolfed it down with a noisy slug from his *Coke*.

Rachel glanced suspiciously into the darkening shadows of the back seat. Tom had always made little slip-ups during his visits where he appeared to be saying things to her grandmother, but he seemed much worse now. She was worried he might have lost his mind or had some sort of stroke since Thanksgiving. She busied herself with another piece of chicken.

By the time the two partners in crime reached the New York State line, Tom's exuberance had given over to paranoia. The ten cups of coffee and quart of *Coca-Cola* he had consumed had plainly contributed to his growing anxiety. He thought he could see unmarked squad cars lying in wait for them at every curve in the road.

Rachel noticed that her grandfather's monologue with the back seat of the car was becoming more intense with his growing exhaustion and agitation.

"I know I didn't mention the name of the town I was calling from to Ms. Ingrahm, Anna. I'm sure Claire always referred to the boat as, *Annie*, just like we do. They'll be searching for a boat named *Annie*, unless Claire had the full name and call sign written down somewhere. Did you or your mother have the name of our boat written down anywhere?"

Rachel appeared to be asleep.

"You don't suppose Sister Emilia got the license number of the car?"

Even Tom had to admit this last possibility was unlikely.

"We're just going to have to keep moving. We'll keep to the gunkholes and run the coast north, instead of south. They'll expect us to head for the keys, Anna, so we'll sail to Nova Scotia instead."

Pleased with this apparent solution to his predicament, Tom relaxed his grip on the wheel enough to take the car into a brief, but terrifying slide along the gravely shoulder of the road. The time was now two-o'clock in the morning—0200 in a sailor's lingo. Tom O'Connor admitted with reluctance that he had to stop to rest.

Rachel awoke as her grandfather eased the car to a stop and cut the engine. They were in the parking lot of a truck stop near Syracuse, New York.

"Where are we?" she asked sleepily.

"Nearly home, Darlin', nearly home," he answered, his voice laden with nervous exhaustion. "Why don't you just crawl into the back seat. You'll be more comfortable if you stretch out."

Rachel peered into the cavernous darkness into which her grandfather had been directing much of his conversation throughout the evening. She hesitated a minute, but then crawled over the front seat and settled in behind Tom.

Dead tired, but unable to fall asleep immediately, Tom sat at the wheel waiting for the tension in his body to ease. Rachel had fallen asleep at once.

"She's beautiful, isn't she?" he said softly, his voice heavy with exhaustion. "Just as beautiful as she was on that first day."

Memories of that unforgettable experience in the birthing room were emerging from the past.

"I guess you're glad we kidnapped her, right?" he asked.

Anna O'Connor was extremely pleased with what Tom had done.

Chapter Five

Tom O'Connor opened one eye. He was lying with the upper half of his body stretched uncomfortably along the front seat of the car. As light flooded his field of vision, he saw an angelic face peering down at him. Was it the face of the wistful angel aboard *Annie?* Tom lay puzzled that he had made it back to his boat so quickly when the eyes in the angel's face blinked, transforming the visage as if miraculously, into Rachel's face.

She was leaning over the car seat looking down at her grandfather. Dawn had broken. There were miles yet to go. Tom regretted there was no place to swim.

Tom struggled into a sitting position, shaking the stiffness from his aging bones. He sat for a moment looking at his granddaughter's face in the rear view mirror.

"Tom?" Rachel began inquisitively.

"You have to go again, right?" he suggested.

"We're in big trouble, aren't we?" Rachel asked directly. Her face betrayed genuine concern. "I mean, you kidnapped me, right?"

"Kidnapped you? How could we kidnap you, when you belong to us already? Listen to this, will you?" he added, directing the remark to the space beside him.

"Will they put us into prison when they catch us?" Rachel asked.

These were serious questions. They deserved serious answers.

After a moment of reflection, Tom turned to confront his granddaughter directly.

"We didn't exactly kidnap you," he began. "They probably would have awarded us custody of you, eventually."

Tom paused. He realized he wasn't coming across with the conviction he was groping for and which the situation demanded. He changed his tack.

"You see, they were planning to conduct a hearing, which is a meeting where a judge, some lawyers, and a social worker get together to decide what to do with young people like you, with orphans I mean."

Rachel nodded. "Orphan" was now a familiar word in her lexicon.

"I guess we were not so certain the judge would award us custody, of you I mean," Tom explained.

"Sister Emilia said I was going to be placed in a foster home," Rachel said.

"See, that's just what we were afraid they might do," Tom said, following his granddaughter's cue.

"Why don't they want me to live with you, Tom?"

"Because I live on a boat rather than in a regular house," he answered, after a moment of reflection. "All we want to do is show the judge assigned to your case that we can get along fine on *Annie*. But as far as prison is concerned, don't you worry about that!"

Tom gave his granddaughter a conspiratorial wink.

"They'll never catch us," he assured Rachel, embellishing his remark with a maliciously boastful grin.

Rachel scrutinized her grandfather's face. Tom looked terrible. She recalled seeing a horrible painting once at the Undergraduate Library on campus at the university. The picture was of Jupiter or one of those other gods. He was eating one of his own children, or maybe his father. Tom looked exactly like Jupiter in that painting with his wild white hair flying uncombed all over his head and his eyes rimmed in red.

Rachel was by no means confident they would not be caught, or that the two of them would not end up in jail.

By 0730, the O'Connors were back on the road, bolstered by a breakfast of bacon, eggs, coffee, and chocolate milk. They had survived a hair-raising incident earlier that morning at the rest stop.

Tom and Rachel were walking back to the car after breakfast, when a New York State Police cruiser had halted not fifty yards away.

Tom had urgently coached Rachel in an anxious whisper to keep walking straight ahead, admonishing her not to betray any signs of the panic he was feeling.

They had almost reached the car when their world had been shattered by a firm command to "Hold it, right there!" The O'Connors had stopped in their tracks. Helpless, they watched the trooper approach. Flight would have been senseless.

The expression of abject fear on Rachel's face seemed oddly comical to Tom. He had done his best to suppress a laugh. There was nothing for it, but to face the music.

"Yes?" Tom had managed weakly, as the awesomely bulky trooper reached them.

"The young lady dropped this," the officer said, handing Rachel a plastic tooth bush holder that had apparently fallen out of the overnight kit Tom had purchased for her.

Tom had been stunned to speechlessness by the apparently miraculous reprieve. He stammered some incomprehensible reply. Rachel had saved the day.

"Thank you very much, kind sir," she said, accepting the lost article with just a hint of a curtsey and a smile that would have melted the heart of an ogre.

The officer had doffed his hat, about faced, and returned to the cruiser without further ceremony, leaving Tom and Rachel weak in the knees.

The remainder of the trip passed uneventfully. The incident with the New York State trooper seemed to belie the likelihood that an all points bulletin concerning the fugitives had been issued by the Michigan authorities. The O'Connors passed over the Piscataqua River just after 1400 and zoomed past the village of Kittery into Maine. Camden was now only 160 miles down East.

At Freeport, the O'Connors exited Interstate 95 and drove into the center of town.

"I didn't buy you any clothes, because I figured you had grown some since I saw you last," Tom explained. "But we'll fix that little problem at *L.L.Bean.*

The salesperson at the *L.L.Bean* factory outlet greeted Rachel and her grandfather cordially, after Tom had guided his granddaughter into the women's clothing section of the store.

"I'd like to see some quality sailing wear for the young lady," O'Connor pronounced.

"I'm sorry, Sir," the salesperson responded, "but we don't carry a children's line.

Tom O'Connor was flabbergasted. He and Anna had been shopping at *L.L.Bean* for almost thirty years.

"You don't carry clothing for children?" he parroted.

"No, Sir, I'm sorry, but we don't."

Tom stood massaging his beard and looking with confusion from Rachel to the salesperson.

"Well, how about showing us something appropriated for a petit woman. You carry small sizes, don't you?" Tom suggested.

"We do," the clerk admitted, "but I don't think that would work out." She was looking to Rachel for support and getting it.

"Why not?" Tom asked ingenuously.

"Well, it's a little hard to explain, Sir, but the problem is the way the garments are cut, you see."

"Let's try a few things anyway," Tom demanded.

The apparel looked great to him. The two females, however, rejected each item as unacceptable. Tom appealed to Anna, but got no support from that quarter either. There were things about women he realized he would never understand.

An hour later, after Rachel had been outfitted at a clothing emporium for pre-teens in items that looked identical to what she had modeled at *L.L.Bean*, he vented his exasperation.

"Can you imagine *L.L.Bean*, our *L.L.Bean*, not having a children's line?"

Rachel shrugged her shoulders. Her mother had explained a few things about men. She was beginning to see that her grandfather was a typical male. Rachel realized that any appeal to Tom's sense of reason would be fruitless. The present situation called for reticence and a few condescending smiles.

Tom exited the Interstate 95 at Brunswick and followed Route One into Rockport, arriving at the *U-Save Auto Rental* just before closing time. The clerk at *Smith's Garage* was astounded at the mileage—free mileage, Tom reminded him—logged in so short a time.

A skirmish ensued when Tom confiscated all of the paper work related to the rental and insisted on paying for the use of the car in cash. After an increasingly heated exchange of words, American greenbacks won the day.

By the time he and Rachel had hiked over to Camden, picked up some supplies, and eaten in town, twilight had fallen. Rachel was subdued as she stepped aboard *Annie* from the pier at *Wayfarer Marine*. Tom was a little disappointed by his granddaughter's lack of enthusiasm for what was now her new home, but he attributed Rachel's tepid reaction to fatigue and the fact that *Annie's* beauty was not fully apparent in the waning light. The sun was now barely illuminating the crests of the Camden hills.

Rachel disappeared into her sleeping bag in the starboard quarter berth—her new bunk—almost immediately. Tom concluded there was nothing for it but to turn in himself.

Tom O'Connor usually slept fitfully in his aft cabin bunk. He had typically tossed restlessly as Anna stood her watches at the helm. Anna herself could have slept through a hurricane.

An old adage has it that the ears never sleep. Such lore is particularly true of a sailor asleep aboard his ship. The sailor's ears are attuned to every familiar sound, the complex audible collective of the internal processes, the breathing, of his ship. But the sailor's ears are even more attuned to any unfamiliar sound. Despite his fatigue from the grueling trip to Michigan and back, just such an unaccustomed sound awakened Tom O'Connor. The sound was soft and muffled, but he recognized it immediately as the sound of weeping.

Tom rose from his bunk and made his way in the darkness to the quarter berth. He lifted Rachel in her sleeping bag and carried her to the aft cabin, where he gently situated her next to his place on the bunk. Rachel snuggled closer to him, as he placed his arm around her shoulder.

"It will be all right," he managed, his own voice breaking slightly as he spoke.

Tom was unable to visualize his granddaughter's face in the darkness, broken only intermittently by the red flasher on Northeast Point. The harbor was still, the foghorns quiet. He could appreciate the ebbing of Rachel's distress, as she snuggled closer, until she was finally subdued by no longer troubled sleep.

Tom O'Connor felt needed by someone smaller and more vulnerable than he was. He was suddenly overwhelmed by a sense of profound and unexpected happiness. Partly conscious, he savored the moment, as his awareness slowly faded. He drowsily monitored each of *Annie's* familiar sounds. Contented, he sensed that all was well. The *Chelsea* timepiece at the navigation station smartly sounded three bells. Tom lay quietly in his bunk beside Rachel, as oblivion slowly erased him.

Chapter Six

Rachel was tentative about her new surroundings when she emerged from the aft cabin just after eight bells the following morning. Tom had been up since dawn. There was a slight chill in the light air coming down off the Camden hills. The dearth of wind offered little incentive to an early departure. Tom had already been topsides. Taking advantage of the water tap at the *Wayfarer* dock, he had topped off *Annie's* water tanks and swabbed her down, to get her looking pretty for her new co-skipper. Tom relished the salty dampness of a typical New England morning on the seacoast. He was very glad to be home.

Rachel, on the other hand, sat forlornly at the saloon table, wrapped in her sleeping bag. She was not a little disconcerted by the recent perturbations in her life. She knew her grandfather had always been strange. Her mother had tried to pass off Tom's quirks as something called "x-centricity." Now that Rachel had spent more time alone with Tom that she had in her entire life before this, she was worried that he might be just plain crazy, maybe from living alone too long.

Rachel surmised that the two of them were in big trouble with the authorities back in Michigan. She could imagine the Mother Superior's reaction. She prayed Sister Emilia had not been beaten. She also found it scary when Tom talked out loud to her grandmother. He was doing that a lot more now than he had ever done in her presence in the past. Could he actually see her grandmother, she wondered?

Still, he was trying to be awfully nice to her. Living on this stupid boat for the summer would *probably* be better than staying in the convent or being sent to an orphanage or foster home.

As she explored *Annie's* interior through her still sleepy eyes, Rachel recalled having been aboard Tom's boat a few times when she had been younger. Her recollection, however, was of a much larger boat. Now, in the cramped space of *Annie's* cabin, she found it difficult to imagine how anyone could possibly live in so small a place. *Annie* was pretty, with everything made of polished wood and brass. She didn't want to think about buffing all of that brass, though. She hoped that was not the reason Tom was so anxious to have her aboard.

The yogurt pancake Tom slapped down before his granddaughter disappeared like the tail fins of a broaching whale—a good sign, he concluded.

"Bet you can handle another one of those," he suggested.

Rachel nodded, but didn't say anything. Despite what Tom thought was a fascinating explanation of *Annie's* interior structural features and equipment, his granddaughter seemed to be on the verge of tears. The most animated response he was able to elicit from Rachel was a lunge toward the second crepe he plopped onto her plate.

Tom effected the galley clean up silently and with dispatch. He brought his third cup of coffee over to the settee and sat down facing Rachel. He was worried. His granddaughter seemed much more withdrawn than she had been during the trip down to the coast. He was hoping her moroseness was simply a consequence of the novelty of her new surroundings. He was groping for some way to break through her reserve, but none of the tactics he had tried that morning seemed to be working.

"So what do I do now?" he asked aloud.

Rachel seemed bewildered by her grandfather's remark. She responded only by peering at the surface of the table as if seeking a place to hide. She wished Tom would stop talking to himself. Rachel was embarrassed when he did that.

An awkward silence followed. Then Tom left his seat and made his way forward to the fo'c'sle, where he extracted an object, meticulously wrapped in plastic, from one of the lazarettes. He returned to the saloon and placed the package on the table before his granddaughter.

"Well, go ahead. Open it up," he prodded.

True to expectations, Rachel was unable to resist. She extracted from its wrapper what Tom considered to be one of the most beautiful objects in the world, the musical jewelry box that had belonged to his wife. He said nothing, as he sat watching his granddaughter. Rachel appeared interested in the little box, but so far she had examined it only with her eyes. Vaguely, in the distant reaches of her memory, she could see her grandmother's pleasant face.

Some seconds passed before Rachel's inquisitiveness forced the issue. She reached out and gently lifted the lid. The mechanical device in the box responded with the refrain of Pachelbel's *Canon in D*.

"All of those things inside belong to your grandmother," Tom managed, "but I suppose she would expect me to give them to you, now that you have come to live with us."

Rachel's eyes met those of her grandfather. For the first time, Tom could read in those eyes the telltale signs of fascination.

For a while longer, Rachel—although intrigued by the contents of the box—did not touch anything. There seemed to be something sacred about the fact that these things had belonged to her grandmother.

Tom reached over and gently examined his granddaughter's ear lobes.

"I seem to recall that your mother had your ears pierced when you were a little bit of a thing, no more than a year old," he said. He extracted in turn the gold posts from each of Rachel's ear lobes, replacing them with an elegant pair of pearl earrings from the box.

Tom rose from his seat again, this time retrieving a small hand mirror from a locker in the heads. Holding the glass before her face, Tom displayed her new adornment for Rachel.

Tom blinked and swallowed hard. He knew that the face peering with subtle feminine approval into that mirror was not Anna's face, but the face of an eleven-year-old girl. Still, he was intrigued by the sensations of pleasure the objects were obviously eliciting—sensations that appeared not to have changed in over thirty years.

Rachel's face betrayed the nascent features of the young woman she would soon become. Her hair was long and golden brown with red highlights. There were hints in Rachel's face of an exotic Middle Eastern beauty that led Tom to speculate that her father might have been Egyptian or Lebanese. For the present, though, Rachel's face was still that of the gawky, freckled, pre-teen her mother had described.

Tom watched with fascination as Rachel began to finger in turn each of the objects in her grandmother's music box. For Tom, each item conjured memories, timeless scenes of happiness and love. As he sat with Rachel that morning in *Annie's* saloon, Tom recalled magical moments in the subdued atmosphere of candlelight, the glow illuminating sparkling glasses of rich, red wine. He was able to relive the vibrant inner touch of giving. He could see Anna's face, its unsullied beauty sensuously aglow with wine, with affection, and with appreciation for the small gifts he had meticulously selected, each imbued with symbolism and unspoken meaning.

When these scenes had dissipated, Tom sat for a while longer, tracing the signs of renewed pleasure the objects where now eliciting on Rachel's face.

Finally, Tom rose and made his way to *Annie's* stereo. He put on a collection of baroque classics and cued up the *Canon in D*.

Rachel O'Connor became as enthralled with the music as with her new possessions. She adorned herself in a lavish profusion of bracelets and brooches, surveying each new effect with a lilting glance in the mirror, as her head swayed to the subtle and haunting refrains of Pachelbel's beautiful masterpiece.

By the time the remainder of the disc had played through, Rachel had reached a state of tranquil saturation with her new finery. Her grandfather leaned toward her. The wind was up.

"What do you say," Tom suggested, "Why don't you and I and *Annie* go for a little sail?"

PART III

RACHEL & ANNIE

Chapter One

The first sail Tom and Rachel O'Connor shared on the *Anna Livia* was a washout. They had just cleared the Graves when the wind died with no fanfare. Dead calm from horizon to horizon befell the sea. Soon there was not a ripple to be seen on the mirrored surface of the ocean.

The O'Connors sat bobbing in the swells for twenty minutes while *Annie's* main sail swapped and rapped like the limp rag it had become. Reluctantly, Tom fired up the iron jib.

Against his better judgement, Tom had monitored the weather forecast that morning. Fifteen knots out of the southwest had been predicted. Listening to the report had been an afterthought, while he scanned the airways for references to a renegade sailboat named *Annie.*

Rachel sat silently in the cockpit, feigning disinterest in her grandfather's tirade about the perversity of somebody named Aeolus and the comedians at the National Weather Service.

Tom grew morose himself as they motored out to the red nun buoy off Robinson Rock. From this way point, he intended to strike off for the Fox Island thoroughfare, the passage that runs between North Haven and Vinalhaven Islands. As the *Anna Livia* rounded the southwest extension of North Haven Island, Tom was thoroughly disgusted by the dismal conditions on this crucial day, especially when he recalled the glorious rail down passages under full sail that he and Anna had made through the thoroughfare in the past.

Still, this was a beautiful New England summer morning. There is always something to be said for the sea and for the beguiling sensation of being upon it in a small ship. Tom extracted some *Ban Soleil* from the cockpit lazarette and dabbed some of the sunblock on Rachel's face.

"Rub that in," he said.

"You didn't think I'd remember, did you?" he asked his ghost with a smirk. He held up the tube of sunscreen and shook it in the direction of the empty space on the starboard side of the cockpit. The application of sunblock had been one of Anna O'Connor's obsessions when at sea.

Within an hour, Rachel was fidgeting from boredom. Tom clipped her safety harness to the port hand jack line and suggested she go forward to explore the foredeck and watch for porpoises and whale. When she returned to the cockpit a short time later, having seen nothing but waves, Rachel was not convinced that porpoises or whale even lived in Maine.

Tom O'Connor had not forgotten the mistakes he had made nurturing Anna's interest in sailing years before. His plan this time was to turn the entire operation of the ship over to Rachel as soon as possible. He decided this was an auspicious occasion to begin Rachel's instruction in the art of small boat seamanship, so he asked his granddaughter to take *Annie's* wheel.

After a simple demonstration of how *Annie* responded to her helm, Rachel proved adept at maintaining a steady course.

"I might have known!" Tom said. "Your grandmother's the best helmsman I ever met, so I guess it would be only natural that you'd have the knack. I've never been worth much at holding courses myself. No patience for it, I guess."

As Rachel held the *Anna Livia* on a steady heading at 6 knots under engine, Tom began working with his granddaughter on the names and functions of a boat's gear and rigging. Total familiarity with the details of a ship's operation is more than just an exercise in nautical protocol.

Safety is an issue too. Every able bodied person aboard a sailing vessel has to know what objects do and what they are called. Rachel was not to be spared the learning of a rigorous catechism of nautical terms. If she ever had to cast off a port hand jib sheet in a hard blow in the middle of the night, Tom wanted to be certain his granddaughter would know how to do that properly.

Part of Rachel's education had to do with aides to navigation.

"Now, you see the difference between cans and nuns," Tom said, pointing out the squared off configuration of the *C-17* can lying just west of the village of North Haven.

"Years ago, cans were black, but now they're green as you can see. Nuns have always been red as far back as I can remember. I could never figure that one out, Skipper. Seems to me the nuns should have been painted black."

Tom's plan was to harbor hop short distances in the beginning of his and Rachel's flight to Nova Scotia. He felt that short periods of time on the water would make ship and crew less conspicuous and less susceptible of detection if the Coast Guard had an alert out for them. He thought it would be safer to hide out in gunkholes for the first few days, unless they happened to encounter some great sailing wind. In that case, Coast Guard or not, *Annie* was going to fly her rags.

For the first time in months, Tom was monitoring the distress and calling frequencies on *Annie's* VHF and single sideband radios. To his relief, there was no indication anyone was looking for them. As a precaution, however, Tom clipped a couple of old beach towels to the stern quarter lifelines on both sides of the boat. The *Anna Livia's* name was thereby obscured from view.

Considering the continuing dearth of wind, Tom decided to round up beyond Hopkin's Point on Vinalhaven Island and put into the anchorage off Perry Creek. With Rachel at the wheel, setting *Annie's* hook that afternoon was a piece of cake.

"Nice to have crew," he muttered to his ghost, with just a hint of sarcasm in his voice.

"I didn't hear you, Tom," Rachel yelled from her position behind the wheel. "Should I shift the engine into reverse?"

"Pay me no mind," he yelled back, feeling mortified that he had confused his new co-skipper with his ranting. "Just follow my hand signals."

Rachel was an extremely quick learner.

"Inherited your brains," Tom whispered beneath his breath. He paid out the chain and then gave Rachel the thumbs down signal. She responded by shifting *Annie's* transmission into reverse, setting the hook nicely.

Rachel could not believe she had actually set the anchor without wrecking Tom's boat. She hoped Tom knew what he was doing. Her head was befuddled by a scrambled mess of terms from aft to abeam, halyards to nun boys.

After taking two deep breaths, Rachel began to relax. She was proud of herself. She had been terrified for a while that she might shift the transmission in the wrong direction and run *Annie* into a rock until it occurred to her that the stupid shift lever moved the same way the boat did, back for reverse, forward for forward. Actually, Tom's hand signals made sense too, if one thought about it. Thumb up for forward, thumb down for reverse, right for starboard, left for port. Rachel was relieved to find that at least some things on a boat were logical. Maybe sailing Tom's boat was not going to be so boring as she had expected.

Annie lay at anchor off the green boathouse on the north side the mouth of Perry Creek. After battening down the sail, winch, and pedestal covers, Tom rowed Rachel up toward the head of the creek. He and Anna had loved this idyllic spot, with its sloping rocks making way inland from the water's edge. Sea bird infested marshes are interspersed between stark stands of pine forest.

"We should be able to get some great mussels here, Skipper," Tom suggested.

The O'Connors collected some beauties that afternoon. Rachel seemed to love the atmosphere of Perry Creek as much as her grandfather enjoyed it. The place is, of course, delightful. Rachel and Tom managed a swim in one of the shallow spots. They whiled away a typical cruising afternoon, rowing to the head of the creek and meandering among the stands of pine and spruce.

They spotted some kingfishers plying the shoreline and Rachel was treated to her first experience of the mysteries that abound along the water's edge. Later that evening, the O'Connors shared their first seafood aboard *Annie*. Rachel had perked up considerably, to her grandfather's considerable relief.

"Some of these mussels contain pearls, you know," Tom remarked casually, as he placed the steaming bucket of mollusks on a trivet on the saloon table.

"Really?" Rachel asked with interest.

"Well, they're not all that big," Tom confessed, not wanting to dampen Rachel's expectations, "but they are genuine pearls."

As they consumed the delicious mussels, dipping them in drawn butter, the dregs of which they sopped up with chunks of sourdough bread, Rachel and her grandfather found four keepers. Rachel stashed these away in the quarter berth in a *Ziploc* bag, together with her new collection of shells and other shore objects.

Rachel's first day aboard *Annie* ended with the sun gently setting behind the pines and spruce of Vinalhaven Island. The trees offered the two sailors a sparkling display of fragmented dancing light. At first mosquito, Rachel and her grandfather ducked below. Rachel turned in early, leaving Tom to his evening readings by the light of the trawler lamp.

"Well," he said, before retiring himself, "what do you think?"

Tom's ghost agreed that Rachel's indoctrination to the nuances of small boat handling was proceeding considerably better than either of them had anticipated.

Chapter Two

A stiff breeze out of the southwest augured well for a better day when Rachel and her grandfather removed and stowed *Annie's* sail covers the following morning. Tom sensed an opportunity to make a rag bagger out of his granddaughter. *Annie's* engine would remain silent this day.

Going forward, he began preparations at the bow for getting underway. The *Anna Livia* was going to sail out of the anchorage at Perry Creek.

"You see that nun off to the northeast?" O'Connor called out from his position at the bowsprit, pointing out one of the buoys lying off Zeke Point. "I'm going to pull your hook, Skipper, and haul your mainsail. You just steer straight for that nun."

"Do you really think I can do it?" Rachel asked hesitantly. Tom was not exactly what most people would call normal. Again, she hoped he knew what he was doing.

"Hey, Anna, listen to this, will you?"

Tom was beaming at Rachel, who looked rather small and less than confident from her perch behind *Annie's* hefty steering wheel.

"Of course you can do it, Skipper," Tom shouted.

Deftly, he cranked up the old *Bruce* anchor. Making his way quickly to the starboard mast pulpit, he raised *Annie's* faded mainsail. The *Anna Livia* paid off smartly and began reaching off to the northeast. Rachel had a death grip on the helm. She was worried stiff she was going to wreck Tom's stupid boat.

"Hey, Skipper, relax!" Tom called out, after checking *Annie's* track. "You're doing fine. Steady as she goes. Just lock on that little red nun."

Tom moved aft and joined his granddaughter in the cockpit. He wanted to let Rachel ghost along under main alone until she became accustomed to the feel of the boat under sail.

When they reached the angulation in the direction of the Fox Island thoroughfare off Fish Point ledge and headed up in the direction of the Goose Rocks, the change in course brought *Annie* closer to the wind. She lay over to port and picked up her pace.

"Whoa!" Rachel cried out, a little panicked by her first taste of heel. "She's tipping over!"

Gently, Tom reassured his granddaughter, explaining *Annie's* need to lay down on her lines in order to achieve what she had been created to do. They continued to sail along under the main alone while Rachel became more accustomed to the helm. Tom began to show her how to pick up navigation aids from a chart.

Tom had an ancient edition of chart 13305 aboard—entitled *Penobscot Bay*. The sheet was frayed and stained, but still serviceable.

"Coastal charts cost a fortune these days," Tom explained. "By rights, we should have the latest editions aboard, but the government has nearly priced these things out of the marketplace. Fortunately for us, the rocks and islands in Maine don't often change their positions."

Tom pointed out the correspondence between their passage over a world on paper and the passage *Annie* was making through the water. The next mark was the *C-5* can off Bradstreet Rock.

Rachel took the chart from her grandfather and studied it more closely. She was able to maintain her track by bracing the wheel with her knees, as Tom had demonstrated. Rachel had about a million questions about the various symbols the chart contained.

"Passages are usually easy, once you get used to reading these things," Tom explained. "Remember, though, if you ever get confused, stop!"

Looking up from the chart to the surrounding topography, Rachel was steadily orienting herself.

"The next mark is the number four nun, right?" she asked with interest. Peering off ahead slightly to port, Rachel spied the small red object.

"There she lies," Tom said in confirmation.

"So what do you say, Skipper, let's bring this pretty lady up to warp speed."

As he left the cockpit to raise the staysail and genoa, Tom cautioned Rachel about the effects the headsails would have on the helm. He also wanted her to be prepared for the additional heel *Annie* would experience once the foresails were flying.

"Now, she won't tip over!" Tom admonished. "Your grandmother didn't convince herself of that for years."

"Got your next mark?" Tom asked.

Rachel checked the chart and gave her grandfather a weak thumb's up sign. Her face did not display much confidence, however. She had no idea what might happen next.

"Okay, then, let's do it."

Tom scampered forward. Checking the sea state, he was pleased to read a solid force three wind—ten knots—in the occasional whitecaps visible off Calderwood Neck. He hauled up the staysail. From his position at the mast, Tom could appreciate a surge of power as *Annie* instantaneously responded. Glancing aft, he could see that Rachel was leaning a little more heavily into the helm. She managed to return his sign of encouragement, accompanying her thumb's up with a weak and sickly little smile.

Tom monitored his granddaughter's reaction intently for a few moments to make certain she was on top of the situation.

"Remember," he shouted, "she won't tip over!"

Rachel nodded, but said nothing. She was hoping *Annie* would not rise up out of the water and fly off into space, like those kids had done on their bikes in *E.T.* Tom's boat was moving very fast.

"Your head sail is going up, Skipper!" Tom cried out. Raising the big genoa had always been thrilling on a day with precious wind. The old tan bark rag almost flew to the masthead and the *Anna Livia* came alive.

"Hey, whoa!" Rachel squealed again, as *Annie* lunged forward into the swells with a new surge of energy.

"Hold that helm, Skipper!" Tom cried out with a laugh, as he dressed and cleated the jib halyard. He was back in the cockpit in time to see the color returning to Rachel's face. He winched in the working genoa sheet, trimming the big sail for maximum thrust.

"Kind of exciting for six miles an hour," he suggested, once the boat had settled into her track.

"Yeah!" Rachel exclaimed. Sailing *was* fun, a whole lot more fun than Rachel had expected.

"Where's your next mark, Skipper?"

Rachel had momentarily forgotten all about navigation. She examined the chart.

"The red nun off the Mark Island ledge, but I don't see it yet."

"Hold her at 090° compass, Skipper," Tom suggested, after eyeballing the course on the chart and factoring in a few corrections for leeway and magnetic variation.

"Aye, aye, Captain!" Rachel said gleefully.

"Watch that now, Skipper," Tom chided, "no fair stealing my lines."

The eight nautical mile reach over to the Mark Island lighthouse proved to be a great introduction to the pleasures of sailing for a neophyte like Rachel O'Connor. Aeolus had served up a perfectly gentle breeze. Tom offered to spell Rachel at the helm, but she gracefully declined. Her grandfather took Rachel's refusal of assistance to be a very good sign.

From the lighthouse, the O'Connors shifted to chart 13313 and headed up slightly into Merchant Row. *Annie* skirted a proliferation of stark white and pink granite islands capped by dark crops of wooded greenery. In Tom's view, Merchant Row is one of the most beautiful places in the world.

The wind held and the five-mile passage through the Row was completed quickly. Leaving the number one can marking Colby Pup to starboard, Rachel next brought *Annie* out into the open waters of Jericho Bay like a seasoned mariner. Give a kid a chance, Tom reflected, and she'll shame the most skeptical adult.

As the morning wore on, Tom subjected his granddaughter to a running banter, reviewing the significance of each of the various symbols on a nautical chart and the correlation between the symbols and the reality they represent. Rachel's head was spinning with new facts, ranging from rocks awash to self-tailing winches, but Tom persisted with a relentless course of instruction.

The conversation had bogged down for a while, however, at a point half way across Jericho Bay.

"Have you ever been to one of the big cities like Washington or New York City?" Tom had casually asked.

"I went to see Washington with Momma," Rachel said in a subdued tone. She could see her mother's eager face, explaining the sights with animation.

Tom winced. He immediately tried to recover.

"The stone in many of the buildings you saw there came from here. Did you know that?"

"No," Rachel responded. Her enthusiasm had been dampened by the recollection of her recent loss.

"Well, it's true," he affirmed. "I think the Brooklyn Bridge was constructed of stone from these islands."

Tom stopped speaking. He looked helplessly at Rachel, who had suddenly become quiet. She seemed to be unduly preoccupied with *Annie's* helm.

"Then the industry just went bust and died out," Tom said softly. "I guess that happens sometimes."

The temporary silence aboard the *Anna Livia* was terminated when Tom picked up the chart.

"Do you have the Halibut Rocks light?" he asked.

"I think I see it right up ahead," Rachel said, with renewed interest.

"Bow on," Tom confirmed. "We'll leave the light and the can north of her to starboard and then shoot the slot between the nun and can leading into Toothacher Bay. You know, beyond the obvious, I have never been able to learn why the bay is called that."

Rachel had a fleeting recollection of her dentist's office, but she quickly drove all traces of unpleasantness from her mind. The islands ahead were beautiful. Sailing was becoming a lot of fun.

Rachel and Tom had logged nearly 18 nautical miles so far that morning. The time was about right for lunch. The wind was beginning to slack off as it often does around midday, especially when it blows out of the southwest.

"What do you say we put into Burnt Coat Harbor on Swans Island?" Tom suggested. There was something special on Swans Island that he had been anxious to share with his granddaughter.

Tom dropped and bagged the genoa as *Annie* came abeam of the can off Gooseberry Island ledge and opened the harbor entrance.

"Swans has always been a favorite of your grandmother and me," he told Rachel, as the *Anna Livia* swept gracefully in the direction of Harbor Island under main and staysail. "We're especially fond of Burnt Coat Harbor.

"The French named the harbor 'Brule Cote,' which translates to 'Burned Coast.' The region had suffered a recent forest fire at the time the French passed through, hence the name. The English alliterated the French 'c.o.t.e.' to 'coat,' and so the name stands.

"A man, who called himself 'King John,' and his wife settled on one of these islands. They had thirty-six children. That's how the entire population of the island got started.

"The name of the island came from a man named 'Swan,' of course, who ended up beheaded during the French Revolution. If you're interested, you can read about this kind of stuff in the guidebooks we have below.

"Anyway," Tom continued, "the Swan islanders are about the nicest people you'll find anywhere. Now, take a look at that chart."

Rachel picked up the 13313 and studied the Swans Island area more closely.

"Do you notice there is no apostrophe in 'Swans'? You know what an apostrophe is, don't you?"

Rachel looked indignant. What did Tom think she was, a kindergartner?

"Of course I do," she said in a huff.

"Just checking," he said, apologetically. "The islanders are fighting with the Coast Guard and the Post Office to get an apostrophe into the island's name in honor of old Swan, but with no luck so far. The opposition thinks the change would be for the birds."

Tom chuckled, but the pun appeared to have been lost on Rachel, who had a pained expression on her face. After his crack about the apostrophe, she was in no mood to give him any satisfaction by laughing at his stupid joke, which really was for the birds.

Fortunately, *Annie* had almost reached the anchorage. Tom began to elaborate the technique of bringing a ship to anchor under sail.

"When I give you the signal, Skipper, just take her up onto the wind and hold her nose right there. Your outstanding crew, that's me, will do all the rest."

Rachel's first hook under sail was an impressive piece of seamanship. She was much more relaxed at the helm by now. Tom appreciated the luxury of an extra set of hands aboard. He made his way back to the cockpit after setting the anchor. He always loved to relax for a moment during that time of grace when one's ship is secured to the bottom of a fair harbor.

"Great sail, hey Skipper?" he suggested with enthusiasm, smiling broadly at his granddaughter.

Rachel was surveying the picturesque ambience of Burnt Coat Harbor. She didn't directly answer her grandfather's query, but Tom interpreted the expression on her face as another good sign. He pointed out the imposing edifice ashore that comprises the *Swans Island Boat Shop*, advertised as the largest wooden structure since the Trojan horse.

Rachel had already picked up much of the routine of belaying lines and replacing the sail covers after *Annie* made port. As a final precaution, Tom readjusted the bath towels that obscured the ship's name. Then he and Rachel boarded the dinghy and rowed into Minturn to the *Olde Salt's Galley* restaurant.

The *Olde Salt's Galley* is a small red clapboard building that makes up in ambience what it lacks in size. Rachel and her grandfather declined a table on the deck outside, having had enough sun for one morning.

"The young lady and I would like a couple of pound and a half lobsters, maybe with a few rolls and some chowder on the side," Tom informed the waitress before she had a chance to present the menu. "Can you handle that?"

The waitress, who was new since Tom's last visit, seemed to be checking him out. He had his hair in a ponytail. The server had noticed his earring.

"Ayeh, we can handle that," she said, flashing Rachel a sympathetic smile.

"Now, you understand," Tom added, "we want those lobsters hypnotized before you submerge them."

The waitress was beginning to look like Jack Nicholson's nemesis in the movie, *Five Easy Pieces*.

"How, pray tell, do you hypnotize lobsters?" she asked sarcastically.

Tom could tell from her affected accent that the waitress wasn't a native Mainer. He launched into an elaborate discussion about the hypnotizing of lobsters, explaining how essential the process is to ensuring perfect flavor. The technique prevents, he explained, the release of the hormones of fear at the moment of a lobster's contact with boiling water. Hypnotism of a lobster is accomplished, he went on, by placing the animal in a three-point stance on its head and outspread claws and rubbing its back, gently.

"Rubbing its back?" the waitress parroted.

"Gently," Tom affirmed. "If a hypnotized lobster's tail fins begin to flutter, that's a sign that it is coming out of its trance and that it needs more rubbing. Now, I've tried lobsters both ways—hypnotized or not—and there is no comparison in flavor."

"We don't ordinarily hypnotize our lobsters, Sir," the waitress related dryly.

Tom began to massage his beard as he peered up at the server from his seat.

"You weren't working here the last time I was in, were you?" he observed. "But that's okay," he conceded, "we'll just head out to the kitchen and hypnotize them ourselves, just like I did last time I was here."

There ensued an altercation, a debate rather, between Tom O'Connor and the proprietor of the *Olde Salt's Galley*, who had been called in by the server to adjudicate. The owner professed no recollection that Tom or any other patron of his had ever hypnotized a lobster on the premises. Arguments were presented about health codes. Bribes were tendered and mutual threats were tentatively made. In the end, Rachel and her grandfather were escorted, reluctantly, to the kitchen of the *Olde Salt's Galley*, where they each duly hypnotized one live pound and a half Maine lobster.

Rachel was reluctant to touch hers initially, suspecting that a lobster's body might be cold and slimy. She was gratified to find this was not the case. Even more impressive, however, was the fact that a lobster seemed to *like* having its back rubbed and was quite willing to remain in a three-point stance until the moment of its execution. The waitress, who had never seen a lobster hypnotized, was amazed that the tail fins actually do flip if a hypnotized lobster begins to recover consciousness. She insisted on being allowed to put Tom's lobster back under herself, the first time the tail fin flipping happened.

Back at their table while their lobsters were cooking, Tom explained to Rachel that hypnotism really does affect the flavor of a lobster, invoking the testimony of his ghost, with whom the process had been thoroughly tested.

"You see, Skipper," he added conspiratorially, "hypnotizing your own lobster also ensures that it is *alive* before it is cooked. Every now and then, some restaurant will try to slip a frozen one in on you, if you are not careful.

Tom noticed a look of consternation on Rachel's face.

"What's up, Skipper?" he asked.

"I'm not sure if I'm even going to *like* lobster, Tom," she admitted. "Sticking mine in boiling water made me feel a little queasy."

"Well, you might not like lobster, I suppose," he conceded. "But don't worry, yours won't go to waste if you don't. I trust then you've never tried lobster?"

"In Chinese food, I think," Rachel said. "It was okay, but I didn't have to watch it crawling around and I didn't have to kill it first."

"Now, that lobster of yours didn't feel a thing," Tom reassured her. "You hypnotized it first, remember? Just try it, but don't eat the crusts," he added with a grin.

Rachel had taken her third bite of lobster. She had drawn butter running slowly down her chin. Suddenly, she shifted into high gear consumption of *Homard Americanus.* Tom had never seen anything like it. That lobster simply disappeared before his eyes, tamale and all.

"What would you like for dessert," he asked, once Rachel had converted her lobster to a pile of crusts and broken claws. He surmised that anyone who was able to put away a lobster with the gusto Rachel had displayed must have a bottomless pit for a stomach.

Rachel had never tasted anything so delicious in her life.

"Another lobster!" she suggested with no hesitation.

"I know, I know—hypnotized!" the waitress conceded, as Tom placed the order for Rachel's second crustacean. Thus was born what would become a family tradition—Rachel O'Connor's "dessert" lobster.

The waitress had warmed to her customers in typical Swans Island fashion by the time Tom ambled up to the cash register to pay the bill.

"You know, I've never known another kid who would eat tamale," he commented.

The waitress shivered, just thinking about the greenish muck that is supposed to be a lobster's excretory organ or liver, or whatever.

"It's rare," she agreed. "We had a kid in here from New York who would eat it about a year ago."

"Well, that's my granddaughter!" Tom said, beaming at Rachel, who was standing beside him with the glazed look of a totally sated lobster aficionado in her eye.

"Ayeh, Pops," the waitress responded, "I didn't think she was your wife."

Chapter Three

Rachel O'Connor was sitting with her grandfather in *Annie's* cockpit. She was wearing her grandmother's tattered oiled wool sweater. With her knees drawn up to her chest, the time worn garment reached to her ankles providing a welcome foil against the chill in the early evening air. A mosquito coil sent a helix of smoke skyward. *Annie* was riding to a rented mooring in Northeast Harbor on Mount Desert Island. For the moment, neither of the O'Connors was speaking, transfixed as they both were by what was happening in the sky.

The cloud formations this evening were alluring. A mass of what Tom explained were mid-level altostratus clouds covered the entire south half of the canopy of sky above them. A triangular wedge of open sky surged upward into this cloudbank from the pine-studded hills of Mount Desert Island. Through this gap, the sun was just now descending.

To the north, the more open sky was peppered with a myriad of discrete altocumulus clouds that hung above the ship like small gems suspended in the hyaline blue of what could only be called that evening, the heavens.

Rachel and her grandfather sat in silent awe as each of the small cloud masses inherited from the setting sun a crescent of brilliant gold at its base. In minutes, color seemed to consume the substance of each individual mass, leaving a sky studded in swatches of richly gilded pigment.

No less impressive, the larger bank of clouds nearer the horizon underwent a metamorphosis of its own to assume various textures resembling a veritable catalogue of priceless fabrics. Some of the formations were gossamer, like strands of hair. Other more solid masses had assumed the consistency of regal brocade.

The celestial pageant evolved as the waning light softened into twilight. The grand illumination of Northeast Harbor spread to burnish the tops of the higher trees. The night sounds of the harbor softened. The O'Connors sat engrossed in the spectacle, until the gallery in the sky slowly faded with the advancing darkness.

The day had been eventful. The wind had come pumping out of the southwest again by the time Rachel had finished her second lobster. Weighing anchor at Swans Island, the exodus from Burnt Coat Harbor had required a short beat down the passage defined by Hockamock Head and the Gooseberry Island ledge to starboard and Harbor Island to port. *Annie's* heading directly into the wind afforded Rachel her first experience bringing a small sailing vessel about. The passage became Rachel's first beat to windward.

"Prepare to come about!" Rachel shouted with excitement as *Annie* came perilously close to danger on her port tack course.

"Ready, Skipper," Tom responded.

"Helm's alee," Rachel informed her crew, laying the wheel over and throwing *Annie's* nose through the wind.

The sails cackled and flapped like a rookery of tormented gulls until, with a smart smack, the genny paid off to leeward. Tom cranked in the jib sheet like a sailor possessed by all the mad devils of the sea.

Tack after tack, they repeated the procedure until they opened Green Island. The track to the south brought *Annie* sufficiently off the wind to allow Rachel to fetch her course close hauled on a starboard tack. She then brought *Annie's* bow to the northeast in order to shoot the gap between Crow and Sister Islands.

The wind had by now veered to the west and was holding at a steady 20 knots, with gusts closer to 25 or 30. The *Anna Livia* was off on what Tom liked to call a "screaming reach." Rachel O'Connor was no longer bored.

"Hold that helm, Skipper!" Tom laughed, as his granddaughter fought *Annie's* tendency to take her bow into the wind during the heavier gusts. Rachel was laying into the wheel with determination and was handling the situation well. Tom had decided not to reef the mainsail, opting instead for a heart-thumping ride downwind ahead of the building swells.

The *Anna Livia* was in her element reaching in a stiff wind before a quartering sea. She was a double-ender. Her canoe shaped stern had been designed to allow her to come into her own in just this kind of following sea. Rail down, she slammed into the troughs. Running at 7 ½ knots, *Annie* was sailing well ahead of the seas breaking behind her. Tom had insisted on safety harnesses for both members of the crew that afternoon.

"The harness is a precaution against rogues," Tom had explained. "Rogues are *big* waves and they're just as mean as their name implies.

"You notice how one of those waves out there—every 7th they say—is bigger than the others? Well, eventually one of them will be much bigger than the rest and that one will be a rogue.

"*Annie* will handle nearly anything, Skipper, but every sailor has to develop a healthy respect for rogues. They can be downright dangerous."

Rachel was searching the surrounding ocean, expecting the worse at any moment.

"What do you do about rogues?" she asked.

"Just hold the helm and nothing bad can happen, except you sometimes get a bath if a rogue decides to come aboard. On a boat like this, rogues are no problem," Tom reassured her, "so long as you and your crew are harnessed and ready for them."

Despite the surly petulance of the waves, Rachel was experiencing for the first time in her life the supreme thrill of sailing on the ocean. She was enjoying herself. She surveyed the seas as they mounted on all sides of her ship. Let the rogues come, she thought to herself. The *Anna Livia* and her crew were ready for anything.

Later that afternoon, the atmospheric pressure tracing on the barograph in *Annie's* saloon began to fall, suggesting the approach of a weather system. Tom also knew that southwesterly winds often bring fog at this time of year. He and Rachel were likely to be socked in somewhere over the next few days. He didn't want to risk being trapped in an isolated anchorage where Rachel would not have much to do. These considerations led to Tom's decision to put in at Northeast Harbor.

One of Anna O'Connor's favorite ports, Northeast Harbor would certainly be of greater interest to Rachel than an outlying gunkhole. Lobster is available and there are several bookstores in town, where Rachel could stock up on some reading material. Tom also knew *F.T. Brown* up on Main Street sells propane, which would allow him to top off *Annie's* tank.

Despite his earlier resolution to keep to the gunkholes, there had been no broadcasts that would suggest the Coast Guard was pursing a boat called *Annie*. A sea town like Northeast Harbor would be safe enough, especially if he and Rachel maintained a low profile.

The decision made, Tom spelled Rachel at the helm. He showed his granddaughter how to plot a course and put Rachel to work determining the track to the South Bunker ledge nun and the entrance into the Western Way. By mid afternoon, co-skipper O'Connor, back at the helm, had successfully sailed her ship through the Way, past Cranberry Island, and on into Northeast Harbor.

By the time the *Anna Livia* had picked up her assigned rental mooring and her crew had dined on clam spaghetti and freshly baked bread, the hour was too late for going ashore. The day had been delightfully fatiguing, a port to port sail all the way from Perry Creek.

There was plenty of time, as is always the case when cruising under sail, to defer some things for another day. And so, Tom and Rachel tidied their ship and then watched the sunset as *Annie* lay to her mooring at Northeast Harbor.

The sunset that evening was the kind that spawned hazy speculations about the origin of the universe and about the time when the ocean was young and the tides immense. The tides had been immense in the distant past because the crazy moon, now suspended like a beacon in the evening sky, had once been so much closer to the earth than any harvest moon Rachel and Tom would ever see.

CHAPTER FOUR

Tom's suppositions about the weather had been correct. He awoke at 0600 to find a deeply falling barograph tracing and a harbor enshrouded by fog. Making his way topsides, he could barely see the ghostly forms of adjacent ships in the soft matutinal light that was bathing Northeast Harbor. *Annie* was soaked in a heavy layer of dew. Tom swabbed her down quickly, removing some of the salt from her decks.

Gossamer spider webs hung from the rigging. Each strand—festooned in droplets of dew—glittered like a delicate diamond necklace. A huge spider, plump as the Wife of Bath and doubtless just as dangerous, had been living in *Annie's* stern light since spring. The creature's elegantly woven deathtrap trembled in the rising breeze.

Retreating below, Tom stoked the small driftwood and coal fire he had ignited earlier in the *Luke* fireplace mounted to *Annie's* forward bulkhead. Rachel gave no sign of stirring yet, so Tom whipped up the batter for some buckwheat pancakes and set the mixture aside in anticipation of his granddaughter's eventual ravenous emergence from the quarter berth.

Tom O'Connor cherished the quietude of mornings like this one. He sat for a moment listening to the cries of a distant gull and to the occasional slap of a wavelet against Annie's hull.

"She did a great job yesterday," he said softly. "I think she's going to be all right."

Grabbing a steaming cup of freshly brewed coffee, Tom polished off the *Liturgy of the Hours* for this day in the latter half of the month of June, a day in the 11th week of ordinary time. He then addressed himself to *Ulysses*, reading a passage from the episode called *Circe*. Recalling the spider web he had examined earlier in *Annie's* cockpit, Tom reflected on the strangeness of the Gods. Athena had made a spider out of Arachne, while Circe had turned the men of Odysseus into pigs.

Rachel finally hauled out of her bunk at 0730, just after a steady summer rain began to fall. Wrapped in her sleeping bag, she made her landfall at the fireplace, Anna O'Connor's favorite spot on cold, damp mornings on the water. She greeted her third day at sea with nothing more enthusiastic than a sleepy stretch and a yawn.

Tom went to work flipping buckwheat pancakes. It suddenly occurred to him that they had not yet decided on a morning potable for Rachel.

"Did your mother let you drink coffee?" he asked.

Rachel looked up at him sleepily, shaking her head affirmatively. "But I don't like it," she added.

"No coffee," he said. "I don't suppose you'd care for a beer, then?"

"Tom!" she groaned, her sleepy face contorted by a pained expression. Tom's jokes were exasperating at times, especially so early in the morning.

"How about a glass of powdered milk?"

"Okay," she said, without enthusiasm.

Tom made a mental note to pick up some of the special milk on the market that has a long shelf life without refrigeration, if he could find any. The rain was pelting *Annie's* cabin top by now, but Rachel's spirits had rallied around her fifth pancake, bites of which she retrieved from a small sea of melted butter and *Lyle's Imported English Syrup*.

"At least she's not going die of malnutrition," Tom commented aloud, amazed by his new co-skipper's appetite.

Rachel chose to ignore the remark, which obviously had not been addressed to her. An awkward silence ensued, until Tom resumed the conversation.

"What we have aboard this ship, Skipper—according to your grandmother—is what she calls a "liberated" labor policy. That means we share all of the chores, as well as the fun. Is that okay with you?"

Rachel nodded.

"Now, you are a mite smaller than me, so I'll swap you anchoring for navigation work," he suggested. "How would that be?"

Rachel was familiar with the concept of "liberation," having been indoctrinated about the injustices of a male oriented society by her mother. Although she was prepared to fight for her rights aboard Tom's boat, his proposal sounded fair. She nodded her agreement once again.

"So you agree, Skipper, with that arrangement. We share and share alike in all of the chores except anchoring and navigation."

"Uh-huh," she assented.

"Good, then you do the dishes, since I just did the cooking!" Tom said with a triumphant cackle.

"Tom!" she began to protest, but then reconsidered. Fair was fair.

"But you have to dry," she insisted.

"That's a deal, Skipper" he said with a laugh, as Rachel headed for the galley sink with a handful of dishes and a theatrically exaggerated groan.

The rain had shown no sign of letting up by the time *Annie's* interior had been brought to Bristol condition by her new team of galley slaves. Rachel's own room at home reflected her philosophy about neatness. The shoals she and Tom had skirted yesterday were less dangerous than the hazards that abounded in her own private space. Still, Rachel had to admit that her usual casual approach to tidiness would not work aboard the *Anna Livia*. "Stow as you go," soon became her motto for survival, with no prompting from Tom.

In preparation for going ashore, Tom rummaged for a few moments in one of the aft cabin lockers. He emerged with a foul weather outfit Rachel was to wear over her sweater and sweats.

"I didn't buy you a set of foul weather gear in Freeport, because I thought these would do fine," he said.

Rachel held up the yellow pants and coat, examining them minutely before rendering an assessment.

"They're too big for me, Tom. I can't wear these!"

Tom was not convinced.

"Your grandmother has kindly consented to allow you to wear her foul weather gear, Skipper," he pronounced flatly. "That is top-of-the-line *Henri Lloyd*—the best on the market. Besides, a foul weather outfit is *supposed* to fit loosely, so you can get warm stuff on underneath."

Rachel could not believe that her grandfather was going to be impossible about clothes again. She remembered the scene Tom had made at the first store he had taken her to—*Jim Beam's* or whatever. Rachel felt that a demonstration would be worth more than words against her grandfather's inflexibility. She slipped into the gear and then sat on the saloon seat, posing triumphantly with the arms and legs of *Anna O'Connor's* foul weather suit hanging limply in space beyond the extent of her own smaller extremities.

"See!" she said, with fire and feistiness in her voice.

"No problem, Mon," Tom retorted. Abruptly, he began attacking the garments with a shears he had retrieved from the nav station. A few quick snips and the alterations were completed.

Next, he slapped an old Nova Scotian tarred sou'wester hat on Rachel's head. Completing the attire, he fitted her out in Anna O'Connor's deck boots, after reducing the size disparity sufficiently by stuffing Rachel's feet into three pairs of heavy woolen socks.

"I'll see to the hems later," he said, surveying his handiwork with satisfaction.

Rachel was by no means enthralled. She sat in a huff for a few minutes, looking at the mess Tom had just made and pondering the best means of jumping ship.

"I am *not* wearing this stuff!" she said, in a tone of voice that seemed to preclude further negotiation.

Tom persuaded her to model the outfit by walking up and down the cabin sole. Rachel complied reluctantly.

"You look terrific, Skipper," her grandfather asserted. "Go take a look in the mirror."

Rachel returned from her survey before the looking glass even more bent on rebellion.

"I am *not* going to wear this stuff in front of other people, Tom!" she flatly avowed.

Forty minutes of dialogue ensued before Rachel would relent. Bolstered by a firm promise that a new foul weather outfit would become the first item on the Northeast Harbor shopping list, she finally succumbed to her grandfather's practical assertion that she had to wear some kind of rain gear on such a dreary day. Her grandmother's *Henri Lloyd's* represented the only wet weather gear presently available. The only alternative for Rachel would be to sit out the morning on *Annie*, while Tom went ashore alone. Her grandfather padded his argument with a promise of ice cream, *before* lunch.

"Okay," Rachel finally consented, "but you promised to buy me new ones!"

"Consider that done, Skipper," Tom affirmed, making a sign of the cross in confirmation of his seriousness.

Rachel and Tom had no sooner rowed the dinghy ashore and purchased the ice cream when—despite the overcast weather—the picture taking began. Every tourist in Northeast Harbor seemed to want a shot of "adorable little sailor," in her "cute little outfit." Contrary to her usual reserve, Rachel melted beneath a barrage of requests for special poses.

An only child and latch key kid from a single parent home, Rachel O'Connor was a sucker for that kind of attention.

Tom worried some about private investigators and cops, but he had to admit that Rachel really looked like something, clomping along the docks with an ice cream cone in her hand, the good stuff in that cone disappearing like a rapidly lifting fog. Maybe the sou'wester hat was *slightly* too big, but the face peering at those fawning tourists over the chin straps of Anna O'Connor's foul weather jacket looked absolutely adorable.

"And you say she actually sails!" said one incredulous mid-westerner. The dear lady didn't seem to be able to get enough shots of *Annie's* nonchalant co-skipper, who was primping and posing like a magazine model.

"Why, ma'am," Tom boomed with pride, "of course she sails. As a matter of fact, she's the captain of our ship!"

"See," he badgered Rachel later. "You look terrific in that outfit."

Rachel was unable to deny at least part of Tom's assertion.

"I still want a set my own size, Tom," she said emphatically.

The rest of the morning was devoted to the mundane shore tasks that cruising sailors need to deal with when in port. Rachel and Tom returned to the rain-drenched dinghy and began hauling things into town. The nearly empty propane tank was toted off to *F.T. Brown* for a refill. The dirty laundry was dropped off at the *Shirt Off Your Back*, a small establishment tucked down a gap between two buildings fronting Main Street. The garbage, which had accumulated while on the hook, made its way to a public receptacle.

"Just think of all this work as exercise," Tom suggested, as Rachel struggled with one of the smaller bags of laundry. "Physical work is good for you."

"I'm too young to be a slave," she responded with a pained expression on her face. "Besides, I don't *need* any exercise."

During the wait for the laundry, Tom took Rachel over to the Chamber of Commerce building at the corner of Sea Street and Harbor Drive, where he bought them both a hot shower.

Rachel—again like her grandmother—was a sucker for hot water. Tom finished relatively early. He waited for his co-skipper in the *Yachtsman's Building*, while Rachel apparently recycled half of the Atlantic Ocean in soap and shampoo.

Her skin slowly assuming the hue of a boiled Maine lobster, Rachel luxuriated in a glorious stream of superheated rain. She was in no hurry to leave such a welcome sanctuary. The hot water heater for the shower aboard *Annie* had packed it in when the boat was only five years old. Rachel could tolerate a swim in a backwater stream, such as Perry Creek, but every time Tom talked about one of his plunges into the more open waters of the Gulf of Maine, her blood congealed and her joints froze.

Tom, leafing through the newspaper with growing impatience as he waited for Rachel, disconcerted the occupants of the lounge when he blurted out: "Just like you, I see. If the temperature of the ocean was 30°s warmer, I'd probably have to trail her off the stern all day on an inner tube!"

"I don't suppose there's a speck of dirt left on you?" Tom asked, when Rachel emerged from the shower building at last.

Tom had seen the expression on Rachel's face on another face many times in the past.

Lobsters and hot showers! Rachel would cultivate a great passion for both of these during her summer on the lam with Tom.

After a lunch on lobster burgers, Rachel and her grandfather visited *Sherman's Bookstore*. Not exactly familiar with the reading tastes of the American pre-teen, Tom was surprised by Rachel's choices. She had developed an interest in the science fiction novels of Robert Heinlein. She told Tom that she had read *The Moon is a Harsh Mistress* at least a dozen times.

Least expected was Rachel's exuberant interest in teen magazines, half a dozen of which she gobbled up, drooling over the cherubic male faces on the covers, as the counter person rang up the sale. *Annie's* quarter berth soon became a picture gallery of squeaky-clean portraits of youthful celebrity.

As promised, Tom offered to buy Rachel a new set of foul weather gear, when they stopped off at *F.T. Brown* to pick up the propane tank. He had to admit that the smaller outfit Rachel initially selected *did* looker better on his granddaughter than the older garb. But then, Rachel had surprised him. Looking from the new duds to the old, she had unexpectedly opted for her grandmother's *Henri Lloyd's*.

Tom surmised that the picture taking enthusiasm had impressed Rachel. Whatever accounted for his granddaughter's change of heart, Tom was pleased to negotiate with the folks at the *Shirt Off Your Back* for some professional alterations on the seams and hems of the old, but still serviceable set of rain gear.

Tom and Rachel stayed in Northeast Harbor far longer than originally intended. A break in the weather might have permitted an earlier exodus. In recent years, Tom had generally experienced a restless need to keep moving. He would finish his business and then set sail at the first fair wind. In the old days, however, he and Anna, would often linger about a good harbor for days, even weeks at a time.

Tom and his granddaughter became a regular pair of tourists as the days in Northeast Harbor passed idyllically. They went on sightseeing cruises of the harbor, embarked on a whale watching excursion out to Mount Desert Rock, hitched a ride out to *Beal's* at Southwest harbor for lobster, hiked around, and generally absorbed the atmosphere of Mount Desert Island. Finally, though, the time came to push on to the north.

Tom set Rachel to work plotting a course for Yarmouth, Nova Scotia.

Chapter Five

The *Anna Livia* set sail for Nova Scotia at dawn, riding a southerly force three breeze out to sea. Tracking effortlessly under full sail, she emerged as if materializing out of nothing from the thick fog bank that clung that morning to the crags of Mount Desert Island.

The excitement aboard the *Anna Livia* was palpable. Rachel, growing more comfortable in her role as co-skipper, issued newly learned commands to her grandfather. Tom responded by parroting her orders in a sailor's lingo.

"Aye, aye, Skipper, hardening your jib sheet and trimming your sails."

"Steady as she goes, Tom," Rachel said with pleasure. She clung to *Annie's* wheel, as the ship surged into the swells with reckless abandon.

After giving his co-skipper a few hours at the helm, Tom engaged *Annie's* autopilot and Rachel locked in the course to the first way point she had plotted on the chart of the Gulf of Maine.

Early in his sailing career, Tom had wanted to be a purist and use celestial navigation, taking sights with his sextant exclusively for determining his position on the sea. He and Anna had used the traditional instrument during their trans-Atlantic passages, but they had both succumbed to the wisdom of adopting more evolved technology for coastal cruising. Tom had installed a *Loran*, a long-range navigation system, at *Annie's* navigation station, and then more recently, a *global positioning system*, or *GPS*.

A *GPS* provides incredibly accurate and continuous position fixes and allows the fine-tuning of a course being steered to any way point during a passage. Rachel had selected a series of such way points along the track between Mount Desert Island and Yarmouth and had programmed them into the *GPS* receiver.

The modern navigation instruments aboard the *Anna Livia* were tremendous tools that added to the convenience and safety of a passage, especially one offshore. Tom worried about his growing dependency on the machines, though. The old *Loran* could back up the *GPS*, if the newer instrument failed, but *Annie* was still dependent on electrical power to keep her navigation instruments operating.

Tom and Anna had suffered a close call when a short in one of the navigation lights had fried both batteries in a thick fog. Fortunately there had been no wind that day; so the ship was operating under engine. The electrical alternator on the diesel was feeding power to the radar and *GPS*, so the O'Connors had been able to make a dangerous harbor under conditions of zero visibility. Once Tom had dropped anchor and switched off the engine, however, all of the electrical systems went out, leaving the ship dead in the water until the short was located and repaired and a new set of batteries hauled out from shore.

A total power failure along the coast of Nova Scotia could be a disaster. The fog becomes so thick at times the old Cape Breton mariners joke about how it is possible to sit on the rail of a boat and use the fog as a back rest. The coast of Nova Scotia is also rock strewn and plagued by strong offsetting currents. A quick look at any chart reveals an impressive array of wrecks, evidence of the treachery of the sea for the unwary.

Tom had not given the least thought to the dangers of coastal cruising before now. With Rachel aboard, however, he was not a little disconcerted to find himself thinking very soberly about untoward possibilities.

After lifting in mid-morning, the fog had closed in on the *Anna Livia* again later in the evening, but not before Rachel had been treated to her first glorious experience of night on the open sea. She was mesmerized as she sat in the cockpit beneath a panoply of stars that seemed close enough to the mast to reach up and pluck like bunches of fruit.

"This place is beautiful, Tom," Rachel admitted, as she surveyed the world around her with the sweep of her arm. Never in her life had she experienced anything so spectacular as the conjunction of night, sea, and sky on this evening off the coast of Maine.

Rachel was also impressed by the greenish track of phosphorescence left in the water by *Annie's* wake.

"The glow is caused by diatoms called *Noctiluca*, which translates "night lights," Tom explained. "The disturbance of the water must turn on their switches, but just wait until fall. The glow intensifies then and the crests of the waves actually appear to be on fire."

"I love the quiet, too," Rachel remarked.

"The quiet is nice," Tom agreed, "but the silence of the sea is deceptive though. If you were to drop a microphone over the side right now, you'd be shocked at what is going on down below us."

"Really?"

"Yep, you'd hear every kind of mewing sound, shriek, and ghostly moan you could imagine. Plus crackles and sizzling that sounds like bacon frying or twigs and dry leaves burning. They say the noise comes from fish called *croakers* or from shrimp that snap their claws together like a bunch of politicians. They don't say much of importance, but they make a lot of noise.

"Then, of course, you might hear the songs of the humpback whale," Tom added.

"My teacher played a recording of whale songs last year," Rachel said. "Don't you think they're sad, Tom?"

"Can't blame them, the way we keep killing them off," Tom commented soberly.

Tom became lost in thought momentarily. He was imagining the savagery of the sea, the teeming life engaged in a brutal struggle for survival below the *Anna Livia* at that very moment. Maybe giant squid and humpback whale were locked in mortal combat. Eating machines, blind phosphorescent carnivores were moving ruthlessly through a perpetual snowfall of living sediment slowly falling to the ocean floor. But the greatest predator of all was the one stalking the creatures of the sea in boats from the surface of the water.

Tom snapped out of his haunting, disturbing reverie

"At least there are some people out there who are trying to save some of the whale," he said with reflection.

By 10 P.M.—2200 in a sailor's lingo—the wind slacked off and the fog returned. *Annie* was still making an acceptable four knots. Because of the reduced visibility, Tom advised Rachel to program a 360° alarm perimeter on the radar, at a range of 10 nautical miles.

As the night wore on, *Annie's* cockpit grew wet, cold, and sticky. The O'Connor's donned their foul weather gear. Without monitoring the compass, Rachel was finding it hard to maintain her directional orientation. Ill-defined objects seemed to be materializing at times out of the murk at the periphery of her field of vision.

"It's creepy out here," she commented, as the ship's clock sounded 7 bells at 2300, "I think I'm starting to see things out on the water."

Tom was well aware how easy it is to become disoriented in reduced visibility at sea. Fleeting shapes do crop up mysteriously above the crests of the lumbering waves. He suggested Rachel might be more comfortable below.

A few minutes later, the radar alarm sounded.

"I can see a target off the stern, Tom," Rachel called up. "About 8 miles behind us."

The *Anna Livia* was tracking parallel to the ferry route between Bar Harbor and Yarmouth. Ferry skippers are some of the best seaman on the water and, although Tom was not concerned about a collision, he decided to bear off to port to avoid a confrontation.

"I think they turned with us, Tom," Rachel reported. Tom checked the radar screen. Rachel was correct. The bearing to the vessel astern had not changed. To his dismay, Tom realized that the *Anna Livia* was being pursued.

He veered off to port another 45°, bringing *Annie* hard onto the wind and increasing her speed. Again, the vessel behind them matched the course change. The pursuer was closing in rapidly.

"Hand me the ship to shore radio, Rachel," Tom suggested. Rachel passed the microphone up to the cockpit and Tom transmitted a security call.

"Securitay, securitay, this is the *Anna Livia, Anna Livia, Anna Livia*, Whiskey, Tango, X-ray 2773." Tom relayed *Annie's* latitude and longitude coordinates as Rachel read them off the *GPS* receiver.

"Vessel approaching my position near the ferry route to Yarmouth, please identify yourself."

There was no response.

Tom decided to heave to. Calling Rachel out into the cockpit, he put his co-skipper to work making proper fog signals with the air horn.

Within minutes, *Annie* was lying nearly still in the water. To his surprise, Tom could see from the radar screen that the vessel in pursuit had also taken all way off and was lying about a mile astern of the *Anna Livia.* Tom and Rachel peered into the murk. Nothing was visible except the arcs of brightness projecting into the surrounding wall of mist from *Annie's* navigation lights.

Tom dashed below for a few minutes. He shocked Rachel when he emerged carrying the *Mossberg* shotgun that was usually stowed forward with the storm sails.

"What's wrong, Tom?" she demanded, unable to hide her growing anxiety.

Tom was not certain himself. Furthermore, the possibilities didn't go down easy. No bona fide commercial vessel would behave like the unidentified blip on *Annie's* radar screen. The vessel lying astern of the *Anna Livia* was playing the kind of cat and mouse game typical of the tactics of the Coast Guard, somebody inebriated or crazy, or the subtle stratagems of pirates.

"Pirates!" Rachel exclaimed, parroting Tom's last suggestion.

Tom was anxious not to alarm Rachel unduly, but pirates on the high seas are a threat, even in modern times.

"Your grandmother and I have seen our share of them—pirates, that is" Tom explained. "They *are* more common in the tropics, but the Gulf of Maine is by no means free of them either.

"Remember that pair in St. Thomas?" Tom asked his ghost.

"Make no mistake, Skipper" he went on, "modern pirates don't look like Long John Silver. The two your grandmother and I ran into in the Virgin Islands were about the handsomest young couple we had ever met. All they wanted, they said, was a ride out to one of the out islands. But no sooner aboard and pirates like those kids would think nothing of sailing offshore with us a ways and then throwing us over the side. When I told that young man that I *knew* he was a pirate, he flipped, but he and his mate didn't get within an inch of our boat."

"So what are we going to do, Tom?"

Tom held up the shotgun to emphasize his point.

"We'll shoot them dead before they can get us," he said with assurance. "There is only one law out here on the sea, and that's the law of survival!"

There was something reassuring in the tone of Tom's voice that mollified Rachel. She pointed a strident blast of the foghorn in the direction of the blip on the radar screen.

Neither Tom nor Rachel had noticed the movement of the vessel in their direction on the radar screen, when the U.S. Coast Guard cutter, the *Mesquite*, suddenly materialized without warning out of the fog. A crew of officers armed with machine guns stood at her battle stations.

The *Mesquite's* powerful searchlights swept *Annie's* decks from bow to stern. The hailing microphone aboard the cutter squawked an urgent, not to be trifled with message.

"Prepare to be boarded, immediately!"

Rachel and Tom sat numbly in the cockpit, stunned into immobility by the abruptness of the *Mesquite's* arrival. Both of the *Anna Livia's* crew feared the slightest twitch might bring a barrage of machine gun fire. This was clearly the most dramatic encounter with the Coast Guard Tom O'Connor had experienced in all of his years at sea.

Tom knew it was his duty to *Annie* to demand a soft boarding with an inflatable dinghy, in order to protect her hull from a bashing in the moderate swells that were running that night. He was damning himself for not speaking up, when an inflatable *Zodiac* dinghy plopped off the stern of the *Mesquite*, saving him the trouble.

But then the situation became unpredictably comical. Three officers wearing life jackets got into the *Zodiac*. But then the commander of the boarding crew inexplicably made a ludicrous mistake. In his apparent excitement to board the *Anna Livia*, the crew leader had violated a simple, but cardinal rule of the sea: "Never release a dinghy's painter from its mother vessel *until* the outboard engine has been started."

Rachel and Tom watched in disbelief as the crew of the *Zodiac* made furious attempts to start the outboard, nearly wrenching the starting rope out of the engine. Despite less than sympathetic encouragement from the men on the bridge of the *Mesquite*, the engine would not start.

Making the situation even worse, there appeared to be no oars aboard the *Zodiac*. Before Tom could make any effort to lend the boarding crew a set of oars from his own dinghy, the *Zodiac* and the *Mesquite* had drifted downwind and had disappeared into the fog.

Rachel monitored the two radar blips until they finally merged into a single blip about a mile downwind from *Annie*. Tom was unable to pick up any transmissions on either channel 16 or the Coast Guard priority frequency on channel 22A. He and Rachel never learned what happened to the *Mesquite*. She may have picked up a priority call on some other radio frequency, or the crew may have been too embarrassed to pursue the *Anna Livia* any longer. In any event, the blip on the radar screen roared off in the general direction of Bar Harbor, Maine, and the *Mesquite* was never seen again by the crew of the *Anna Livia*.

Tom was thankful the boarding had been aborted. He suspected the *Mesquite's* mission had been a routine drug surveillance operation. Still, Tom was convinced that he and Rachel were better off not having a Coast Guard record of their names, position, and next port of call on file.

Chapter Six

The remainder of the sail into Yarmouth was uneventful. The fog lifted the next morning, facilitating harbor entry under full visibility. Rachel O'Connor was now a veteran of her first offshore passage. Tom and his co-skipper set *Annie's* anchor and then rowed into the quays of Yarmouth, one of the Canada's salty and quaint little port towns. They celebrated the success of the passage with a huge breakfast of eggs and Canadian bacon, of course, at one of the diners up in the village a few blocks from the wharves.

After debating the wisdom of doing so, Tom dutifully reported to Canadian Customs. The *Anna Livia* had not been tagged a renegade vessel. After the mandatory customs inspection, Tom and Rachel were granted permission to spend the summer sailing the rugged coast of Nova Scotia.

After spending a few days regrouping and provisioning in Yarmouth, Tom and Rachel began to harbor hop the coast, moving steadily toward their ultimate destination, the town of Louisburg, on Cape Breton Island. The province was as delightful this season as it had been on Tom's previous visits.

It is easy to immerse oneself in maritime history along this starkly bare and lonely southeast coast of Nova Scotia. The ghosts of Champlain and the victims of innumerable shipwrecks seem palpably present in the wind that shrieks among the rocks with eerie poignancy.

Rachel and her grandfather put in at Shelburne Harbor, where Tom renewed his acquaintance with "Saint" Harry O'Connor, Vice Commodore of the local yacht club. Tom explained to Rachel that Harry O'Connor is absolutely the most helpful harbormaster anywhere on the coast of North America, and not because of his distinguished name alone. Saint Harry proved his reputation by hauling in diesel fuel to top off *Annie's* tanks, "just in case," and by picking up a couple of lobster culls for Rachel. Culls have a claw missing, making them unsuitable for the commercial market.

Rachel was coming into her own as a sailor by now. Intellectually sharp, she continued to impress Tom. She had most of the nautical terminology memorized. More important, she was beginning to show a giggly enthusiasm for the magic *Annie* could conjure when she did her tricks with the wind and the waves.

Like her grandmother had been, Rachel O'Connor was impervious to seasickness. Tom had tried to rile her up by relating an old anecdote about *mal-de-mer*. The Nova Scotian fisherman like to test a tenderfoot's susceptibility to the malady by cutting out and eating the eyeball of a cod fish, as the neophyte looks on in disbelief. If the newcomer can handle that without losing his cookies, he is welcomed aboard. Rachel had shuddered in response to the tale, but then she had looked Tom mischievously in the eye and had challenged her grandfather.

"If you eat the first eye, Tom, I'll polish off the second."

Leaving Shelburne, the *Anna Livia* skipped Liverpool, making instead for Port Medway. Tom read Rachel guidebook accounts of the settlement of Port Medway by the descendants of families who had sailed on the *Mayflower*. With a sense of envy, Tom read of the proficiency of one John Hopkins of Port Medway who was allegedly able to determine his position in fog by pressing his ear to the deck and listening for the sound of the surf.

Annie's mast height precluded a passage through the Crooked Channel that winds between the islands in the vicinity of the LaHave River, so the O'Connors struck offshore again from Port Medway. Their destination twenty nautical miles down the coast was the port town of Lunenberg. The regrettably short run required to fetch the harbor became one of the most delightful passages of the entire summer.

The conditions the O'Connors encountered could not have been more perfect on that day in early July, when Rachel piloted the *Anna Livia* out of Port Medway and turned her loose like a restless mare on the back of a force five sou'wester blow. The sun was sparkling off the rocky crenulations of a majestic coast. The atmosphere, free of fog, was charged with turbulent energy. Rachel, for the first time since her abduction, was singing at the helm.

At 7 ½ knots, the passage was over all too quickly. Still, there are precious moments in life, some of them sadly shared only by a fortunate few. The powerful, screaming reach of the *Anna Livia* along the southeast shore of Nova Scotia that day in July was just such a boon for Rachel and Tom O'Connor.

As if the sail itself were insufficient, the O'Connors were also afforded the rare privilege of bringing their sleek and Bristol vessel into the magnificent harbor at Lunenberg under sail. The terminus of *Annie's* near perfect flight down the coast was an event crowned in unmitigated splendor.

Rachel brought *Annie* up onto a beam wind as the harbor mouth opened. Her ship responded with a surge of power as it began to track the passage between Battery Point and Kaulback Head. As the *Anna Livia* drew closer, the village rose up before the transfixed crew like the picture postcard Epiphany it becomes from this perspective.

"There lies the port, the sails bloom, as the ship leaves the dark, broad sea," Tom crooned, as the village drew near.

Tom O'Connor had loved this harbor entrance as much as any he had experienced in his years at sea. As the old fishing town materialized majestically above the wharves, Tom recycled memories of the great times in the past when he had walked those quays with Anna. His nostalgic enthusiasm melded with that of the young neophyte aboard, who appeared equally in awe of the scene unfolding before her eyes.

The totality of the thing brought both of the O'Connors to a keen edge of excitement. Abeam of Kaulback Head, Tom doused the genny, but *Annie* continued tracking straight toward the wharves at 4 knots.

"Take her all the way in, Skipper," Tom shouted from the mast pulpit. "Let's show these Canadians some Yankee seamanship!"

Rachel was weak in the knees with exhilaration. Sailing the *Anna Livia* under conditions like this was terrific fun.

"Aye, aye," she yelled.

There was not a quiet heart aboard, as *Annie* made directly for the center of the harbor. Her tan bark sails, old as they were, were gleaming in the sunlight. Her brass appointments were glinting as if afire. Binoculars ashore were already trained upon this stately Yankee sailing vessel making its proud, almost arrogant, entry into Lunenberg Harbor.

Tom, his system surging with Adrenalin, gave a silent, but only momentary, prayer asking forgiveness for the sin of hubris. He sensed, in his pride, how spectacular the *Anna Livia* looked that day, a small sailing ship of impeccable line, with the *Stars and Stripes* streaming off her backstay in the wind.

The plan was to bear down on the wharf until the last possible moment and then head up sharply to fetch the anchorage in the Western Basin. Tom knew the tactic was foolhardy in many respects, but he was feeling young and reckless. He was determined to pull the maneuver off. Rachel was holding the helm steady as a rock, perhaps bolstered in her own courage by the innocence of youth.

The *Anna Livia* surged ahead until—at the last possible moment—Tom gave the signal. Rachel threw the helm hard over to port, taking *Annie* to weather. The ship settled into a breathtaking and powerful track, sailing close hauled in stately beauty parallel to the wharf, which was by now swarming with spectators, who were standing in awe on the quay in poses of envy and respect.

The *Anna Livia* sailed close hauled, pinching the wind all the way into the anchorage, as Tom made his way to the bowsprit. Rachel then put *Annie's* nose hard to the wind, checking her forward progress. Tom dropped the hook and the thrilling maneuver was accomplished, a perfect harbor entry and anchorage under sail.

Tom was still breathless with excitement when he reached the cockpit, where he high-fived his grinning granddaughter. Rachel was still jittery herself, her skin crawling with nervous excitement.

"Great sail, Tom!" she squealed. "Now *that* was a great sail!"

"You hear that, Anna?" Tom shouted. "You hear that? Your granddaughter thinks we played a little music on the rags today. By God, we've made a sailor out of her at last!"

Tom O'Connor's vulnerability for what then happened was predicated most on the fact that Rachel's remark was totally unexpected. Appropriate as it doubtless was, he received it unprepared. He was pumped up, exuberant, maybe happier than he had been in years. The incongruous expression on Rachel's face did not register at first. This expression was not in synch with Tom's own emotional state at the moment. Consequently, when he finally noticed the concern playing across his granddaughter's face, the perception stopped him dead in his tracks. He had no time to let the emotional high ease off before receiving the shock and anguish of an unanticipated blow.

Rachel, from her own perspective, was unable to explain later why her words had surfaced so unexpectedly at that particular moment. In a wrenching spasm of emotion, they had simply poured out.

"It frightens me when you talk like that, Tom," she blurted out in distress. "Grandma is *dead*, Grandpa," she quickly added in a softer tone, her voice edged in anguish. "She's dead, Grandpa, just like Momma!"

His granddaughter's words pierced Tom like a sabre thrust. He was stunned. He was stunned by the import of what Rachel had said. His body slumped against the cockpit coaming.

Tom O'Connor was in Lunenberg, Nova Scotia, his favorite sea town in the world. There were brightly colored buildings rising gently up the hill from the water's edge. This was the home of the schooner, the *Bluenose.* He had just experienced the most spectacular harbor entry he had ever accomplished and yet something was suddenly dreadfully wrong. Tom's breath was being choked off by an incongruous and morbid fear, more terrible than he had experienced in years. He realized he had suffered such an emotion only once before, years ago in Barbados, but he could not allow himself to dwell on the connection. The anchor needed tending.

"Yes," Tom said aloud, "the anchor needs tending."

Time had passed. Tom O'Connor was sitting astraddle of *Annie's* bowsprit, toying aimlessly with the anchor rode. He had set the nylon spring line. The mirrored surface of the water in Lunenberg Harbor was now still. Hardly a ripple disturbed the quietude of a sea now at rest. The glorious wind that had carried the *Anna Livia* so gracefully into port had gradually subsided and had then died off completely.

Now, as he sat alone up forward, the black pool beneath Tom seemed to be the very image of the abyss. He had been staring into this symbolic nothingness during the hour or more than had passed since the incident in the cockpit.

Tom knew of course that his wife was dead. He had always known this, but the delusion that his partner and soul mate still existed in some way, that she was still accessible to him, that he could communicate with her, had afforded him comfort in his inconsolable grief. His delusion was not easy to part with.

Rachel's well-intended and innocent remark had shattered the façade of unreality Tom had been hiding behind. The more realistic grief he was now experiencing was embittered by a sense of waste and failure.

How terribly he had neglected Claire and Rachel. Tom, in his sorrow, realized for the first time that had his wife really been able to communicate with him, she would have castigated him for his selfishness. His ghost had not been the spirit of his dead wife, but a personification of his own vanity and conceit.

Rachel remained alone in *Annie's* cockpit, watching her grandfather as he fiddled with the anchor rode at the bowsprit. Her eyes were brimming with a complex mix of emotion, part sadness and guilt, part anger and fear. How could she have been so stupid? How could she have said something so dreadful to Tom on this of all days? She knew she had ruined everything. She expected her grandfather would return to the cockpit at any moment to announce his intention to pack her off to Michigan on some airplane.

Rachel had never known her grandfather before this cruise had begun, but now that Tom had become a part of her life again, the one thing of which she was most certain was that she did not want to lose him again, not ever.

For a long time, Rachel was afraid to move. She had wrecked the best day of her life and—she suspected—one of the best of Tom's also. She was not anxious to add to the damage she had already inflicted on him, but finally, her suspense about what Tom was planning to do with her became unbearable. Rachel recalled the lessons her mother had often conveyed about the art of dealing with men. If she was going to win Tom back, the situation called for decisive action.

Tom O'Connor started. Rachel had joined him at the bowsprit, but he had been unaware of her approach until she had slipped her arms around his neck.

"It's all right, Grandpa," she said softly. "We have each other now. And we have *Annie*."

As Tom clung tightly to his granddaughter's arms, he emptied himself of many painful aspects of the past.

Some time passed before Tom felt capable of speaking, but finally he turned and was able to confront his granddaughter. Rachel was wearing Anna O'Connor's oiled wool sweater, which was now her favorite garb at sea. She reminded him so much of Claire at that age, as she sat quizzically studying his wrecked face for hopeful signs.

"You know, Skipper," Tom said finally, in a coarsely nasal tone, "they have this restaurant in town called the *Blue Nose Inn*, where we can get Cape Breton oysters, lobster, scallops, clams, and almost anything else you can imagine ever lived in the sea.

"The place is just a few blocks up into town. What do you say we go buy out the kitchen?"

Rachel's smile said everything. She looked like Claire, all right, Tom mused, as he rose to his feet. As he stood for a moment looking toward the wharves, the subtle magic of Lunenberg came drifting over the harbor to reassert itself in his mind. Once more, as if a veil had been suddenly lifted from his eyes, Tom seemed to sense the old familiar charms of this village he had always loved.

Far off, gulls were protesting some grave injustice, but the waning sun was beginning to gild the architectural features dotting the high ground up in town. A soft tintinnabulation of bells echoed in the distance. The sea had become a placid, tranquil thing, as had an old sailor who no longer felt lost and alone.

Chapter Seven

Following the incident at Lunenberg, Tom felt as if a weight had been lifted from his shoulders. His sense of the loss of his wife was still poignant, but he found he was able to deal with Anna's death on a more realistic level since Rachel's intervention. He could not explain entirely why his granddaughter's explicit statement of the obvious had had such an impact. Perhaps he had been moving toward a resolution of his grief unconsciously for some time. Whatever the reason, as he and Rachel explored the southeast shore of Nova Scotia in the weeks ahead, Tom O'Connor began to enjoy himself.

From Lunenberg, the *Anna Livia* continued to run down the back of the prevailing southwesterly breezes, alternating passages through the winding inshore channels that skirt imposing reefs and shoals, with stirring runs outside on the open ocean.

The days rushed by, fusing into a kaleidoscope of cruising experiences. Moving steadily to the northeast, the O'Connors visited the picturesque town of Chester, dug clams at Meisner Island, and speculated with awe about the ghost ship, the *Young Teazer*, in Malone Bay. Tom and Rachel divvied up, in their imaginations, the vast treasure Captain Kidd is said to have left buried on Oak Island.

Rachel ate three lobsters at *Shaftford's Lobster Pound* near Hubbard's Cove on Saint Margaret's Bay. She and her grandfather spent a few anxious moments until their mutually confirmed sighting of the legendary sea monster that frequents these waters turned out to be a floating rubber inner tube. They anchored at Roque's Roost and were fogged in at Terrence Bay, where the *White Star* liner, the *Atlantic*, had struck Mars Head on April Fool's Day in 1873, with great loss of life.

While the *Anna Livia* lay fogbound at Terrence Bay, Tom read John Galsworthy's story, *The Apple Tree*, to his granddaughter. The story was buried in one of *Annie's* musty, salt stained volumes. Tom had always been impressed with the dreadful sadness of the tale.

"Well, what do you think of it?" he asked, after placing the book behind its lee rail.

"That guy was dumb, that...what was his name?"

"Frank Amhurst."

"But Megan was dumb too!" Rachel added abruptly.

"Why do you say that?"

"Because Momma taught me that no woman should ever kill herself over any man!"

The virulence of Rachel's reaction jolted Tom, coming from someone he had assumed to be socially naïve.

"So, do you believe in the Gypsy Bogle?" he asked, to change the subject.

"At one of the witch covenants Momma took me to, the witches said spirits like that Bogle are all around us."

"So your mother was a practitioner of witchcraft?" Tom asked, saddened momentarily by the many aspects of his daughter's life he had been unable to share.

"She was not a *bad* witch," Rachel explained. "Momma believed in Wicca witchcraft. We would go out into the woods and Momma would pray to the mother goddess of the earth. We would make circles on the ground and stuff. It was real nice being out in the woods with Momma."

The sadness in Rachel's face passed quickly.

"At the covenants, some of the other witches would bring their daughters too. We all had a lot of fun, but I never saw anything like a Gypsy Bogle out there in the woods."

Moving on to Halifax, the O'Connors haunted the provincial capital like typical tourists. They visited Historic Properties, the Citadel, and the replica of the schooner, the *Bluenose*. Tom rented a car and drove Rachel down the coast to Peggy's Cove, one of Nova Scotia's most famous tourist attractions, but with a harbor too small to get *Annie* into safely.

From Halifax, the southeast shore becomes progressively remote and desolate. Tom and Rachel anchored above Mussel Island in Sheet Harbor and then ducked into Pope's Harbor. From the latter, they hiked three miles out of town to visit *Willy Krauch's Smokehouse* in nearby Tangier, where Rachel added smoked eel to her growing inventory of the gastronomic delights of the Atlantic seaboard.

By this time, Rachel had made a good deal of progress "learning the ropes." She had mastered the reef knot, rolling hitch, and finally the bowline.

"Did I ever tell you the ropes and lines on *Annie* are alive?" Tom asked one day, as Rachel sat in the cockpit concentrating on the sailor's age-old litany used to properly tie a bowline:

"The rabbit comes out of its hole, sees the hunter, ducks under the log, and jumps back down the hole."

Rachel looked up at her grandfather, breaking her absorption in the spare piece of line she had been working with.

"Tom!" she said with exasperation. "Quit teasing!"

"Who's teasing?" he persisted. "You know about possums, don't you?"

Rachel was becoming accustomed to her grandfather's tactics. Although she might have preferred to ignore him, Tom managed to draw her into the game most of the time.

"Possums?" she responded tentatively.

"How they *play* possum, I mean."

Rachel looked up inquisitively. The connection between ropes and possums was not immediately apparent.

"Yeah," she admitted.

"Well, these ropes here are distant relatives of possums. All they do all day is lay around on a boat playing possum."

"Tom!" Rachel said in exasperation. "Can't you ever be serious about anything?"

"I am being totally serious, Skipper," he protested. "These ropes consider themselves prisoners on boats, you see, and they will try to jump ship if they can. As the next best thing—just to get even with us because we shanghaied them for duty aboard—they come to life and twist themselves into every kind of tangled up mess whenever they can.

"They only do that when you and I are not looking, of course" he added in a conspiratorial tone.

Rachel leered up at her grandfather, acting more frustrated than she actually was at his continual joshing.

"You just keep a close eye on these ropes, Skipper," Tom admonished. "You'll see."

On many occasions in the days ahead, *Annie's* ropes did act as if they had lives of their own. Tom laughed at his co-skipper every time a line tied itself into knots, entangled itself perilously around one of Rachel's ankles, or tried to make a hasty exit through one of the scuppers into the sea.

During the passage out of Pope's Harbor, Rachel's port jib sheet twisted into a tangled mess akin to a pot of clotted spaghetti. Tom whispered to her from his seat at the helm, as if to keep the rope from hearing him.

"See what I mean?"

Tom cut off Rachel's ruffled response with a shake of his head and an admonishing finger to his lips.

"These ropes get mad as hell, Skipper, if they hear you talking about them. You know we can't risk a mutiny"

When the *Anna Livia* reached the delightful harbor at Liscomb River, Tom and Rachel took a "shore break." While *Annie* swung to a rented mooring, Tom and Rachel reveled in the luxury of rooms at the *Liscomb River Lodge*. Here, Rachel renewed her love affair with unlimited quantities of hot water, while adding planked whitefish to her growing list of seafood favorites.

While at anchor a week later north of Misery Island in Country Harbor, the *Anna Livia* sustained an efflorescence of insect life, the occasional bane of the cruising yacht. Tom and Rachel awoke one morning to find *Annie's* decks darkened by a coating of miniscule winged animals, which had exuded a profusion of eggs and spawn during the night. Rivulets of light green slime were oozing toward the deck scuppers.

An exasperated Rachel O'Connor, furiously swabbing the decks, "casually" broached the general subject of bugs.

"Where do all of these things come from, Tom?"

Looking toward the relatively distant shoreline of Country Harbor, Rachel added vociferously. "How can bugs this small fly so far? Or do they walk over?"

As Rachel hauled bucket after bucket of seawater aboard, in a concerted effort to flush the scuppers free of bug spawn, her grandfather opined that spiders, flies, and other members of the phylum of insects generally arrive on boats by air.

"You're kidding me again, right Tom? Spiders don't even have wings!"

"They don't?" he said, feigning ignorance of so profound a fact.

Rachel flashed Tom one of those penetrating looks of total disdain that he was beginning to love so well.

"Actually, the upper wind currents carry them along. I read somewhere that spiders have been captured three miles or more above the earth."

"Well, I wish they would land someplace else!" Rachel exclaimed, as she flushed a few million *potential* insects, together with a few thousand *actual* ones, out of *Annie's* port deck scupper into the serene waters of Country Harbor. Beneath the surface, a host of open-mouthed, scaly creatures lay in wait for a breakfast of manna from the skies of fish heaven.

"Especially little green bugs!" Rachel added, with a deft flourish of her mop.

Tom was sitting in the cockpit, his body loosely draped over *Annie's* helm. He was monitoring Rachel's insistent purification of the *Anna Livia's* despoiled gelcoat.

"Have you ever considered," he said reflectively, "what their existence must mean to them?"

Rachel stopped swabbing and looked at her grandfather. She had learned that when Tom asked a question in that tone of voice, the answer was likely to be weird. Rachel was also aware that she need not answer. Her grandfather was about to launch a dissertation.

"I don't care what their existence means to them. I just want them off of my boat!"

"True enough," Tom said with a bemused expression on his face, "*Annie* is certainly your boat.

"You see, Skipper," he continued, "I read a book once by a fella named J.T.Fraser. He defines the term *umwelt* as the sum total of the awareness of any living creature. The *umwelt* of those little bugs represents the totality of their perception of their world. Anything outside of their *umwelt* does not exist for them. Since you and I most likely lie outside of the scope of their awareness—outside of their *umwelt*—we don't exist for them either."

"Umvault, somersault," Rachel declared. "I wish they didn't exist for me either!"

"You see, they don't conceive of themselves as little, or green, and certainly not as bugs," Tom suggested. "Those are qualities, you might even call them limitations, that our species has *inflicted* on theirs."

Tom paused long enough to let his granddaughter chew on this idea for a moment. Rachel realized that her earlier supposition had been correct. Tom was about to suggest something outrageous.

"What I'd like you to do," he advised, "is think about the fact that you and I have an *umwelt* too. Our *umwelt* comprises the totality of the conception we have of our world too. Got that?"

Rachel nodded weakly, but affirmatively.

"Well, the *umwelt* idea raises the *possibility* that we can't see the entire world that exists around us anymore than these bugs can. We think that our *umwelt* is far richer than that of these little bugs. But it is certainly conceivable that there are beings surrounding us right now—let's call them *angels*—whose *umwelt* is as proportionately greater than ours is, as our *umwelt* is greater than that of these bugs. Perhaps some of these beings, whose plane of existence is so much greater than ours is, are observing us right now, without our being aware of their presence. The relationship between these angels and us would be analogous to that between you and me and these little guys. Comprende?"

Rachel was engaging in a slow dance with the yacht mop. She did not respond, but she was interested in what Tom might come up with next.

"We humans, over the centuries, have tended to dismiss the existence of things that don't make rational sense to us," Tom elaborated, "but this idea of different *levels* of awareness—a hierarchy of *umwelts* that doesn't necessarily culminate in our own—opens up all sorts of possibilities for us, Skipper. Maybe entities like angels and gypsy bogles really do exist. Maybe heaven even exists. Of course, we would have no more conception of what any of these things were *actually* like than these little green bugs have of you or me."

Rachel O'Connor was convinced that her grandfather was about the strangest man she would ever meet, but part of what Tom was saying made sense.

"Who knows, Skipper, maybe there isn't even any death," Tom concluded, embarrassed by the betrayal of emotion these last words conveyed. He recovered and then paraphrased the uplifting ending of the *Brothers Karamazov* more forcefully.

"Maybe it is true what they teach us in religion. Maybe we shall all rise again from the dead, and will see each other again, and tell each other with joy and gladness all that has happened."

"You mean like Grandma and Momma?" Rachel suggested, tentatively.

"I mean like your grandmother and your mother, Skipper."

"Do you really believe that, Tom?" Rachel asked. "I mean that there *really* are angels, and stuff like that, and that we'll really see Grandma and Momma again some day?"

Tom O'Connor looked into his granddaughter's eyes. He saw reflected there the innocent skepticism of the modern age, softly effaced for the moment by the potential for hope.

"Yes," he said, without equivocation, "I *really* do believe that."

The moment passed. Rachel returned to the swabbing of *Annie's* decks, but with considerably less intensity than before. She was feeling more sympathy for the fate of slimy little green bugs.

While in the Country Harbor area, Tom renewed his acquaintance with Murray George—the bootlegger at Drumhead—whose wife, Martha, served up a batch of cod fillets, with a mess of cod cheeks and cod tongues on the side. Rachel's usual voracious appetite for these delicacies resulted in a good deal of chiding from Martha that Mr. O'Connor could not possibly be feeding the child enough. Tom simply smiled, gave Rachel a knowing wink, and made no comment.

Martha George doted on Rachel, treating her like the granddaughter she had never had. Naturally, Rachel melted under a barrage of attention. Mrs. George was a fourth generation Nova Scotian fishwife, whose husband had only turned to bootlegging because poor health and hard times had driven him off the fishing fleet.

Murray George was a sickly, wizened man in the late stages of emphysema. He huddled near the wood burning stove every evening promptly at sundown, where he sat chain-smoking cigarettes.

There is something exquisitely different and pleasurable about the ministrations of another female, Rachel observed, as she compliantly submitted to Martha George's slow stroking of her hair with a hand brush. They were sitting before the mirror in the room Martha—insisting that the O'Connors remain ashore as houseguests—had assigned to the younger of the two visiting seafarers.

"You can stay on that boat of yours anytime, Mr. O'Connor," she had remonstrated, when Tom tried to gracefully decline the invitation. "Lord knows you will probably die aboard, but this young lady needs a good night's sleep in a proper bed for a change."

One look at the mountainous feather bed that was to be her haven for the night, and Rachel enthusiastically concurred, not bothering to mention she had spent a night in the *Liscomb River Lodge* not that long ago.

"I knew your grandmother back in the old days," Martha George related, as she brushed the last tangles from Rachel's hair. The sudden audible inspiration of breath that preceded most of her remarks, a typical Nova Scotian linguistic trait, fascinated Rachel.

"I think Mrs. O'Connor was one of the most beautiful women I ever saw, and she was nice, too. I mean she never flaunted what she had, thank God.

"They were a wonderful couple, your Grandma and Granddaddy," Martha George continued. "I envied them both, of course, being able to cruise around the world on a fine looking yacht.

"They were on their way to Ireland when we first met them. I don't think I have ever seen two people their age so much in love and so full of life.

"I just couldn't believe it when your Granddaddy came by this way after the Mrs. had passed on. That was three, maybe four years ago. I never saw such a change in a man. He hardly spoke more than a word or two, if that. Mr. George had to drag him off that boat of yours. I doubt he would have come ashore, otherwise. He was just visiting all of the old places, you see."

Rachel had not known her grandmother long enough to have any meaningful memories of Anna O'Connor, other than of the photographs in her mother's albums. She had been less than three years old when her grandparents had left for Europe. Somewhere, in the depths of her past, there was a woman, idealized over the years, and known only as "Nanny." Rachel could not be certain whether this vague image was any different than the fairy godmothers and good witches imprinted in her mind during her childhood.

"I will say this, though," Martha George concluded, just before she tucked Rachel in. "Your grandfather seems a mite better off now than he was the last time he set down in the harbor. But then, I suspect, you had a lot to do with that."

Later, as she lay in comfort beneath Martha George's goose down quilt, Rachel tried to materialize a clearer image of her grandmother, but she could not embellish the face now frozen in old photographs. Anna O'Connor had been lost to her somewhere in the distant past.

Suddenly, Rachel was overwhelmed by the sadness of all such losses. Tears welled into her eyes.

"I miss you, Momma," she whispered into the darkness.

But then, as the terrible emotion washed over her, Rachel reasserted herself. She refused to succumb to such thoughts of sadness and loss. The painful sensation ebbed, replaced by images of Tom, who was not an old rascal by any means. She envisioned *Annie* lying safely at anchor not far away. She recalled the exquisite taste of cod cheeks and the warm sensation she had experienced at the gentle hands of Martha George. Rachel's last thought, as she settled into sleep, anticipating the grand breakfast Martha had promised, was a curious thought. Rachel's thought had something vaguely, but very importantly, to do with angels and little green bugs.

Chapter Eight

From Country Harbor, Tom and Rachel sailed the offshore route to Cape Canso, preferring to dodge the hazards of the inside track. Rachel loved to sit at the bowsprit, as the sea miles passed beneath *Annie's* hull, watching the ship overtake legions of jellyfish, the quiet flowers molded by the sea, as the creatures leisurely followed the plankton steadily shoreward.

Sightings of whale are infrequent, but always electrifying experiences. On this passage to Cape Canso, a humpback broached 500 yards off *Annie's* starboard beam. Fear, tempered by resignation, gripped the crew of the *Anna Livia* as the creature made straight for them, sounding only at the last possible moment, or so it seemed at the time. The majestic form swept visibly throughout its length with breathtaking presence beneath *Annie's* hull, before passing on to some more important rendezvous somewhere far away.

Rachel was capable of plotting an accurate course by now. She picked up the crucial navigation aides at White Point, Cape Breaker, Grime Shoal, and then guided *Annie* through a pea soup fog under radar, from the outer harbor light into Canso Harbor. Tom set the hook between George and Piscatique Islands.

Tom had always considered Canso Town one of the most dismal harbors he had visited. Despite its rich history and importance to the Nova Scotian fishing industry, there is a certain ill-defined bleakness to the place, especially evidenced by the stark waterfront conglomerate of corrugated steel fish sheds that comprise the *Canso Seafood Company*. Were it not for the supermarkets on Water Street, the movie house, and Canso's location as a jumping off point for a crossing of Chedabucto Bay, Tom might have been tempted to bypass the place.

Rachel, too, was unimpressed, the more so when the O'Connors learned the movie house had closed since Tom's last visit.

Leaving Canso with no regrets, the crew of the *Anna Livia* rode a fair tide and fair wind across Chedabucto Bay to Cape Breton Island. Rachel picked her way through the traffic separation zone that directs heavy shipping through the Straits of Canso. Visibility was acceptable on the day of the crossing. *Annie's* encounters with three of the big tankers was less traumatic than Rachel had expected.

Annie's course next skirted the industrial coast that extends northeast of Port Hawkesbury. The ominous stacks of the power plants in this area, despite their barber pole décor, seem incongruous with the pristine natural beauty of Cape Breton. Notwithstanding their utility, the huge industrial complexes seem to symbolize the defilement of a bleeding environment for the crass purposes of economic exploitation.

Rachel and Tom spent nearly two weeks exploring the anchorages tucked away in and around the Lennox Passage and Ile Madame. Acadian French influence is strong in this region, as evidenced by names such as Arichat, Cap Rouge, Port Royale, and Ile Madame itself. Typical of the experiences of the entire cruise thus far, Tom and Rachel spent one pleasing day after another trudging the intertidal zones along mile after mile of rugged, nearly deserted beach.

On one of these junkets along the shore of Janvrin's Island, Tom witnessed a rite of passage. Watching his granddaughter as she stood upon a knoll with the wind in her face, sensing the salt smell of the sea spray and the sea wrack, Tom could read in every aspect of her demeanor that Rachel O'Connor had fallen irretrievably in love with the sea.

Of the living creatures of the North Atlantic, the most intriguing are the ubiquitous sea birds. Puffins, loons, and gulls abound. Tom shared with his granddaughter the strange lore of marine birds. They tested the contentions that a certain indescribable cry of the loon, or the sight of gulls flying close to the surface of the water, augurs rain. The old mariners also insist that gulls swarming inland in flocks foretell a coming storm, or that birds visible high above the mast of one's ship signal the coming of wind. Tom and Rachel found such adages more likely than not to be true.

Watching the antics of sea birds in the isolated anchorages of coastal Cape Breton, one can become convinced that gulls *are* the souls of old sailors frequenting once more their favorite haunts. Or that *Mother Carey's Chickens*—black birds with white patches near their tails, also known as *Leach's petrel*—just *might* be the souls of those lost at sea.

The old timers also claim that crows flying across the bow of a ship foretell the coming of misfortune. Andre Boudreau, of Arichat, affirmed the truth of this bit of sea lore. Mr. Boudreau rowed out to visit the O'Connors in a punt, as the *Anna Livia* lay off the *Le Noir Museum* in Arichat Harbor, on Ile Madame.

Old Andre had a wild look in his eye and an expression on his face too weird to make him dangerous, Tom concluded. After delivering his message about the crows, he had added mysteriously: "You notice there are no trees here about."

Tom was aware that the original trees on Ile Madame had been used in building Nova Scotian schooners, but neither he nor Rachel could see any connection between the absence of trees and crows. Mr. Boudreau did not elaborate. Instead he tossed an object into *Annie's* cockpit.

"Present for the young lady," he explained, after the fact.

Old Andre's gift was a hissing, squirming, and particularly horrid specimen of eel indigenous to the area, one of those strange, astonishing, demon faced, gaping wretches of the sea. The creature was close to five feet in length. Its neck was swelled like the hood of cobra. The eel seemed as outraged as the O'Connors that it had been cast aboard the *Anna Livia*.

One look at the eel and Rachel was suddenly half way to the mast pulpit, having rocketed out of the cockpit in a movement reminiscent of the way frightened penguins leave the sea, like missiles launched from submarines.

Andre Boudreau, having introduced himself, seemed pleasantly amused by the havoc his gesture had caused. Without further ado, he mumbled another warning about crows flying across the bow. Then he rowed off toward the government wharf. Although the crew of the *Anna Livia* was suddenly anxious to move on to Louisburg, Tom dispatched and skinned the intruder. With a certain diabolical pleasure, Tom and Rachel dined that evening on succulent, char broiled eel.

A day and a half later—the season now ten days into August—the O'Connors made the harbor at Louisburg. *Annie's* hook was set off the *Lobster Kettle*, Tom's favorite seafood restaurant along the entire Atlantic seaboard.

First on the agenda, however, was a trip out to the museum, *Fort Louisburg*, where Rachel dutifully presented her entrance visa from the King of France to the heavily armed guard stationed at the gate. This imposing personage—probably a student from *Dalhousie University*—played his role to perfection, demanding that Rachel speak French, of course.

Once inside the fort, it is easy to drift back in time to the 18th Century. Rachel and her grandfather topped off the morning with a period lunch in an Inn, dining on pewter dishes filled with beef stew and with slabs of rich black bread, which had been baked that morning in the fort's own bakery.

The *Anna Livia* was now lying just south of the 46th parallel of north latitude. Already, a decided briskness in the air called for daily use of

Annie's bulkhead fireplace. Fortunately, with the cooler weather, fog was becoming less frequent. Tom surmised that they had six premier weeks of early fall cruising still ahead. But clearly, the time had come to reverse course and begin the more rigorous journey south.

The *Anna Livia* would be sailing into the prevailing southwesterly winds between Louisburg and Yarmouth. Steady forward progress would require a good deal of tedious beating to weather. Tom felt the time was now auspicious to finalize his and Rachel's plans for the coming winter.

For her part, Rachel could hardly wait to get back to school. She was starting junior high school this fall. If that was not exciting enough, she realized she had been having the best summer vacation any kid her age could possibly imagine. She couldn't wait for the day one of her unsuspecting new teachers handed out the assignment: "Write a paper on how you spent the summer."

Rachel had been meaning to talk to Tom about where they were going to live during the school year, but they had both been so involved in the boat, the subject had not come up. As far as Rachel knew, the condo in Ann Arbor belonged to her now. She was not sure how she felt about living there, but it would be great to have her own room again, somewhere. Maybe Tom would advise her to sell the condo.

For some time now, Rachel had given no thought to the fact that her grandfather had kidnapped her. As she began to think more about school, however, she began to wonder if her abduction would have any lasting consequences.

Tom and Rachel were sitting on the sun deck attached to the *Lobster Kettle*. *Annie* lay at anchor 300 yards offshore. Neither of them was able to contain the pride they were feeling in response to the comments being made by their fellow diners about the impressive American ship lying in the harbor.

The *Lobster Kettle* looks like the old fishing shack it once had been. Weather-beaten siding on the exterior of the building is unrelieved, except for a red wooden lobster logo and a simple sign confirming the place is open for business. Inside, the no frills motif continues.

Rachel readily agreed with her grandfather that the *Kettle's* seafood chowder *is* the best anywhere, as advertised. She had selected three 1 ½ pound lobsters from the ocean fed holding tank. The ill-fated crustaceans had been duly hypnotized inside one of the *Kettle's* woven net steaming bags and had made the plunge into lobster heaven.

Tom and Rachel were polishing off the last of the chowder, restless as usual during that 15-minute eternity required to properly prepare North Atlantic lobster. Rachel was in animated good spirits, still reveling in the trip out to the fort, a junket that had occupied much of the morning and afternoon.

"Wasn't that *Micmac* warrior awesome, Tom?" she suggested. "Gosh, he was a fox!"

Tom smiled. Rachel looked vibrantly healthy relative to her appearance that day he had absconded with her from the convent nearly two months earlier. She had gained weight and appeared to have grown an inch or so. Her face was tanned and her eyes were alive with enthusiasm and zest for life. The transformation from her earlier taciturn demeanor was gratifying to behold. Tom realized the summer cruise had been good for his granddaughter.

"I'm going to write a terrific report on this trip as soon as I get back to school," Rachel avowed. "I'll bet you I get an A+ on it, Tom!" she added with assurance.

The remark jolted O'Connor. He and Rachel had not discussed the issue of school before this. He suddenly realized he and his granddaughter had been operating from a mutually exclusive set of assumptions about the future.

Tom had naturally assumed that Rachel would continue her education through one of the correspondence courses available to cruising kids. Rachel's comment made it obvious she was anticipating a return to a shore based school in the fall.

"You know, Skipper, we need to talk about that—about school, I mean," he suggested tentatively.

"Great!" Rachel responded. "I've been meaning to ask you when we would be returning to Michigan."

"To Michigan?" Tom parroted. He was nonplussed by Rachel's assumption.

"Yeah, I start seventh grade this year at Pioneer Junior High."

Tom could sense a confrontation in the offing.

"You know, Skipper," he said, "I'm not sure we can go back to Michigan."

Rachel considered a moment.

"You mean they would arrest us?" she suggested.

"Possibly," Tom responded.

"Well, I guess I could go to school somewhere else."

"I was thinking that we could send away for some correspondence courses, so you could go on with your education right from *Annie*," Tom suggested tentatively. "I could help you with your lessons," he added.

"But, Tom, I want to go to school with other kids, just like I've always done!" Rachel protested.

O'Connor sat watching the signs of distress on Rachel's face. He would not have hurt his granddaughter for the world. He could sense her inner turmoil. She looked as if she were about to cry.

Fortunately, the *Kettle* staff called the O'Connor's number. Any further discussion of school was curtailed for the moment by the arrival of the lobsters.

Tom felt he had to try to resolve the conflict later that evening, after he and Rachel had returned to *Annie*. There was a chill in the early twilight air. As Rachel listened, Tom patiently outlined his own plans. They would continue moving south, heading for the Florida Keys. He tried to convince Rachel that enrollment in any land based school would require sending for her academic records. Perhaps a birth certificate would be necessary as part of the application process. He tried to persuade his granddaughter that it might be difficult, if not impossible, to obtain these official documents from Michigan, without divulging his and Rachel's whereabouts to the authorities.

With a jolt, Tom was force to admit, under his granddaughter's interrogation, that similar documents might be required by a correspondence school.

The magnitude of his rashness was beginning to dawn on Tom. He was forced to admit that he had not thought the consequences of Rachel's abduction through with much deliberation.

Rachel remained adamant in her opposition to any of Tom's proposals. She broke down and began to cry, for the first time since that initial lonely night aboard *Annie* in Camden.

"I don't want to live on a boat for the rest of my life, Tom!" she managed. "I want to go to junior high school, just like normal kids do!"

Rachel terminated any further discussion by stomping down the companionway stairs and disappearing into the quarter berth.

Left alone in *Annie's* cockpit, Tom felt unaccustomed apprehension. He seemed to be a million miles away from home, but with no concise idea where home had ever been. The mix of emotions he was experiencing contained a disconcerting sense that Rachel was rejecting him in part, in addition to rejecting the style of life he felt he could never relinquish.

He sat watching first star—*Sirius*, near the constellation *Orion*—as it appeared in the southeastern sky over the quiet town of Louisburg, but he was soon too chilled to remain topsides any longer. He ached for Anna's presence. He would have given anything to have her advice and counsel. But he realized now that she was no longer available to him as before, even in his imagination. There was nothing left of her now, but the bittersweet memories that were forever cascading through his brain like breaking waves on some desolate shore.

Seeking solace in his books, Tom followed his granddaughter below.

Chapter Nine

With a definite sense aboard that the cruise had nearly ended, the crew of the *Anna Livia* reversed course at Louisburg and began the long slog back to Yarmouth. Moving tenaciously against the prevailing winds, the stiff climb to weather required tack after tack through the nose of seemingly hostile breezes during mostly offshore passages.

Tom and his granddaughter utilized every occasion when the wind was fair to move to the southwest. Still, the progress was agonizingly slow. The *Anna Livia* and crew spent several soggy days weathered in.

Night or day, whenever possible, *Annie* would groan into or glide along with the wind. When becalmed offshore, the ship would lie hove to, the crew catching a little sleep on the four-hour watch system Tom had established.

The *Anna Livia* finally left Cape Canso astern. Then she inched back along the southeast coast, making the 180 nautical miles from Louisburg to Halifax in seven rigorous days.

Rachel's mood was one of restless anticipation. She seemed buoyed up by her conviction that *Annie* was finally going home. She was by now reacting to the ship with rote precision. Tom was humbled by his granddaughter's proficiency. Rachel's accomplishments this summer had convinced him he had been correct to push her to the limits of her capabilities.

The issue of school had been left tactfully on the table, a final decision postponed by mutual agreement.

The *Anna Livia* picked up a stiff nor'wester off the backside of a cold front near Pennant Point. The O'Connors bypassed Lunenburg and opportunistically rode the force five blow over a hundred miles down the coast to Cape Sable, covering the distance in a little under 16 hours.

Running before following seas under clear skies all that night, Tom continued to wrestle with what had become an impasse. As he worked though his options from every conceivable perspective, he was unable to come to a resolution of his dilemma.

At times, the problem looked ridiculously simple, the solution obvious. He had an obligation to his granddaughter. He had assumed responsibility for her future. Therefore, the only proper thing to do was establish a land-based center of operations to be used during the school year. They could cruise during the summer. To do otherwise, was selfish. The case, from this perspective, seemed open and shut.

But Tom was not sure he could give up his life at sea. Could he ever stop cruising this unforgettable and slowly moving ocean? Had its currents not entered his bloodstream? Was he completely wrong to feel so defensive about his unconventional life style? Tom had witnessed the resilience and fortitude Rachel had developed during the short period they had been together on *Annie.* Should the benefits of an alternative life style for his granddaughter be so glibly dismissed? Might he not be selling Rachel short by succumbing to her wish to remain in a traditional school system? Could he place his granddaughter behind the ivy-covered walls of some exclusive private school and simply go his way without her? Not likely, he conceded.

Rounding Cape Sable Island, the wind suddenly shifted. Tom brought *Annie* abeam of a heavy and sultry wind blowing steadily from the south, the kind of wind a sailor dies for when moving west. He *was* moving west, in Joyce's parlance toward the realm of the dead. Would he become sere and withered, a yellowed leaf, the mere ghost of himself if he returned permanently to the western shore ahead?

Tom peered up into the silent, unheeding reaches of the sky.

"Give me a sign!" he uttered with frustration, but the universe of transcendent beauty above him was quiet. *Annie* offered no cryptic hieroglyphics in the phosphorescent traces flowing off her stern. The dolphins and the whale were sleeping. The angels, ghosts, and witches of the sea held their tongues.

Chapter Ten

NOAA Weather Radio was predicting the passage of a cold front, but the storm was not expected to reach the Atlantic coast for at least 36 hours.

Tom was monitoring the weather forecast on *Annie's* VHF radio. He and Rachel had just weighed anchor in the harbor at Yarmouth and were underway, bound west-northwest for Mount Desert Island, Maine. The southeast winds predicted for the next 24 hours would be acceptable for reaching comfortably over to the coast of the United States.

The cold front, which had spawned in the Midwest and which had been moving steadily toward New England over the last few days, was of little concern to Tom O'Connor. Neither he nor Rachel had much stomach for waiting the system out in Yarmouth.

The barograph tracing was steady, the wind was right, and the sky was clear as Tom and Rachel sailed *Annie* past the fairway buoy off Cape Forchu and came on course. They were soon reaching under full sail in a force two wind on the beam, making an acceptable 4 knots.

Rachel was in charge of navigation. She was below, checking her charts. Tom smiled to himself. Rachel had learned more about sailing in the two months they had been together than he and Anna had been able to stuff into their aging brains in years. Such is youth, he mused, as he set the controls on the autopilot.

Tom did not see the flock of black birds that passed across Annie's bow. What he did see terrified him almost to the point of turning back, however. A small black bird lying beak down in the water swept past *Annie* on her starboard side. Tom shrugged off what he might have interpreted as an ominous omen.

"The red *8B1* buoy off Baker's Island lies 89 nautical miles ahead, on a course of 289° true, Tom," Rachel called up from the navigation station. "If we can average 4 knots over the water, we should make port in 22 hours."

Similar to the strategy they had used earlier in the summer on the passage from Maine to Nova Scotia, Rachel and her grandfather had timed their departure to give them a daylight landfall on Mount Desert Island. 22 hours elapsed time for the crossing of the Gulf of Maine would put them safely into port well in advance of the approaching weather system.

Beating the storm into harbor was important, not only to avoid the foul weather the front would bring with it. An expected wind shift to the northwest along the trailing edge of the front would bring the wind bow on for whatever remained of the course into Northeast Harbor. An uncomfortable slog to weather on the final leg of the passage was a contingency Tom wanted to avoid. He and Rachel had had enough hard beats into head winds coming down the coast of Nova Scotia from Louisburg.

Tom sat in the cockpit watching Yarmouth recede beneath the horizon off *Annie's* stern. The *Anna Livia* was reaching nicely on a port tack, trimmed and Bristol, right on course. The swells were gentle, rising and falling in a slowly undulating rhythm. The ship was tracking a peaceful sea. If the ocean was aware of its defilement through the agencies of the human spirit, it gave no hint of animosity on this day.

Twelve miles out, the *Anna Livia* swept past the Turcher Shoal buoy. The miles were passing quickly. Just after lunch, the wind began to pick up, but the sky remained clear and the barograph tracing was stable.

Annie responded to the increment in fuel. By early afternoon, she was making 5 ½ knots through the water, a little less over the ground.

The hours that afternoon passed quickly, as they usually do on the open sea. By dinner, *Annie* had logged 42 nautical miles, nearly half the distance to Mount Desert Island. If conditions held, *Annie's* crossing of the Gulf of Maine had every indication of becoming the kind of passage a sailor brags about around a fire in some yacht club ashore.

But conditions did not hold. Tom had seen the state of the sea and sky change abruptly many times in the past. He was not concerned when the wind began to stiffen as twilight fell onto the now agitated surface of an awakening sea. *Annie* began to lay her lee rail into the troughs of the swells, prompting a reef in her main.

When the reef proved ineffective at controlling *Annie's* strain, Tom and his granddaughter harnessed up and went forward to haul down the genny, replacing the big headsail with *Annie's* smaller working jib.

After raising and trimming the smaller foresail, Tom was concerned to see a mountainous wall of ominous clouds rising from the southeast horizon. With darkness approaching, the sun—which had just disappeared in the northwest—was illuminating the head and anvil top of a massive thunderhead, embellishing the crown of the cloud formation with an aureole of golden fire. From the head, flashes of lightning were descending into a darkening wall of eerie green weather.

Throughout the summer, Rachel and Tom had encountered their share of heavy weather, but the atmospheric display this evening on the open sea was one of arresting beauty. Both O'Connors stood transfixed at the mast pulpits for a few moments, watching the approaching storm cell with reverential awe.

"You'd better go below, Skipper, and break out the foul weather gear," Tom suggested. "It looks like we have one coming in."

As Rachel scooted through the companionway hatch and headed below, Tom tied a second reef in the main and dropped the jib to the foredeck. Under double reefed main and staysail, *Annie* had ridden out many a summer thunderstorm in the past. Cells like the one about to overtake her usually blow through in 20 minutes or so, with winds that top end at 35-40 knots. "The sharper the blast, the sooner it's past," is an old sailing adage.

The barograph tracing had been rock steady all afternoon and Rachel confirmed there was no obvious downturn now. The main body of the storm was not due until late the following day. Tom concluded *Annie* had been caught by a local cell, a freak thunderstorm on the extreme leading edge of the incoming system.

With the foredeck work completed and the jib securely stowed, Tom made his way to the cockpit and took a peek below. Rachel handed up his foul weather gear, but she seemed more interested in the radar screen for the moment.

"Look at the size of it, Tom!" she said, pointing out the patch of variegated green shadows on the display. The radar image defined an impressive thunderstorm, larger than any disturbance the crew had encountered that summer.

By range and bearing, Tom estimated the cell would reach them in twenty minutes. Something about the situation made him feel uneasy. Maybe it was that damn bird in the water, he surmised.

"I think we're going to play this one safe, Skipper," he said.

Tom quickly donned his foul weather pants and slipped on his deck boots.

"I'm going to drop the sails. We'll ride this one out under bare poles."

Rachel flashed her grandfather a thumbs-up sign of agreement.

"Can I help?" she asked.

"No, but I'll tell you what. You get your wet weather gear on and break out the life jackets, just in case. And don't forget to clip the safety lanyard to your jacket. If you come topsides, I want you tethered to the jack lines.

"I'll be right back."

One look at the sky convinced Tom he had made the right decision. A stifling greenish-black miasma seemed to have invaded the southeastern quarter of the horizon. The wind had died off completely. The calm before the storm, Tom surmised. *Annie's* sails were flapping idly. Despite the dearth of any local wind, the thunderstorm was racing toward the *Anna Livia.*

The white caps raised earlier by the prevailing wind were now dancing in confused patterns. *Annie* was lurching drunkenly as the seas broke irregularly around her. She was doing battle with the scudding swells, as the storm darkened the dimly lit sea.

Tom clicked the carbine hitch of his safety tether to the port hand jack line and hurried to the mast. As he reached the spar, the encroaching darkness of the early evening ignited in an ominous flash. A brilliant shard of jagged lightning wrenched into the sea with a strange hiss not far away. A deafening clap of thunder followed. The aftershocks rumbled over the ship like the breaking crests of waves exploding on an unexpected shoal.

Tom, occupied at the mast with freeing up the staysail halyard, did not see a second jagged bolt of lightning strike the water a hundred yards off.

His ears ringing with thunder, Tom looked skyward. He was stunned to see the masthead aglow with eerie green phosphorescence. He was thinking about Saint Elmo's fire and how rare it is to see such a phenomenon at sea. He was contemplating calling Rachel up to see the strange atmospheric effect when—like the staggering experience of Saint Paul on the road to Damascus—Tom O'Connor's world disintegrated into an all consuming white presence and then simply disappeared. Tom's last thoughts were of Blake's "shattering glass and toppling masonry, the ruin of all space and all time in one livid final flame."

Chapter Eleven

Darkness had fallen. Tom was disoriented. His consciousness seemed to be fading into and out of a nightmare from which he could not awaken. He was aware of pain in his chest that was so extreme it stifled his breath. He could not be certain whether he was alive or dead.

Tom sensed that he was hanging, gibbeted perhaps. He thought he could make out fires in the distance. A roaring sound in his ears seemed a cacophony of voices, the voices of witnesses to his execution, or perhaps to his burial.

He was able to breathe only slowly, but as he did so he could hear himself emitting a rasping sound. He tried to make sense of what had happened to him. He could only be certain that he was hanging, pinned against a wall, suspended above an abyss.

Tom tried to touch his face. He was able to move his right arm and hand, but he could appreciate only numbness where his left upper extremity should have been. He could not feel his legs. He suspected he had suffered a stroke.

Tom could vaguely make out his right hand. He brought the fingers to his face, but the feel of them was wooden. He explored his face and then his chest, but as he did so his pain intensified and stifled his breath. He began to explore the tether from which he was suspended. As his fingers raced impatiently over what felt like a carbine hook, his situation suddenly became obvious. He was hanging along the side of *Annie's* hull in his safety harness.

As dawn broke in the northeast and a matutinal soft light settled over the sea, Tom's predicament became clear. He recalled the greenish glow of Saint Elmo's fire at the masthead, followed by the sudden flash of incandescent light. *Annie* had obviously taken a lightning strike as the thunderstorm passed overhead, a chance and random event, statistically rare, but devastating in consequence. He had fallen or had been thrown over the side. Tom soberly realized he had been badly injured. After several futile efforts, he found he had insufficient strength to haul himself back aboard with his good right arm. He tried to call out, but he could not get enough breath to make an effective sound.

Directing his attention to the water, he could make out his legs as they trailed limply through the water. But then, he was seized by the terrifying realization that *Annie* was still tracking though the ocean. He had not been able to douse her sails before the lightning struck.

From her angle of heel and depth in the water, Tom was certain she was not taking on water. Fortunately, her through hull fixtures had not blown out, as sometimes happens when a ship takes a lightning strike. But his conviction that his boat was not sinking did little to assuage Tom's apprehension. His mind raged through the horrifying possibilities that now confronted him.

He could not be sure of *Annie's* heading. At any moment, one of the numerous shoals that lay in wait for the unwary mariner along the rock-strewn coast of Maine might rise up to claim its latest victim. Should she run hard aground on a rocky ledge, *Annie* would be mercilessly ground to pieces in minutes. She would join her hapless sisters as an ignominious wreck, claimed by a ruthless and unforgiving coast.

Tom O'Connor would die on the loathsome wreck of the *Anna Livia* and share the shame of fellow mariners, who in times past had also lost their precious vessels to stupidity and the vagaries of an uncompromising sea. Soon, the rocks would claim them all: Tom, *Annie*, and Rachel.

Rachel!

His granddaughter's name seared through Tom's heart, draining him of any remaining will to survive. The only conceivable circumstance worse than the bitter ending that was about to consume him and his boat, would have been Tom's personal survival of such a disaster while losing his granddaughter overboard to the sea.

As dawn broke with subtle mockery, Tom reluctantly allowed his imagination to ramble through the probable course of the preceding night. Rachel had obviously come topsides when the lightning had struck. Not finding him on the boat, she had probably panicked. Tom could envision *Annie's* track through the surging wind and building seas. Knockdowns into the troughs must have occurred, anyone of which might have pitched Rachel over the side.

Tom tried to force from his mind a horrible image of his granddaughter's face. He could not expunge the expression of terror he imagined on the face of an innocent being lost at sea. How long had she floundered, all hope receding as the ship from which she had been so cruelly separated sailed away from her into an eternal night?

In frustration, anger, and despair Tom pounded against the side of *Annie's* hull until his remaining strength failed completely.

Sapped of all will to live, Tom let his body sag limply into the harness. He submitted passively to the judgement of the unforgiving sea. The vanities and stupidities of his life mocked him. He hung like the incautious victim he had become, awaiting the rock that would bring his just and deserving end.

Chapter Twelve

Some hours later, fog engulfed the *Anna Livia*, reducing visibility to a few hundred feet. Tom strained into the wall of haze surrounding his ship. He thought he could see nebulous figures in the murk, the dead fisherman of Gloucester, or sailors lost off schooners on the Grand Banks of Newfoundland.

Tom strained to listen, expecting at any moment to hear surf breaking on the crags of Mount Desert Island. At times, he thought he could hear strange unearthly cries in the distance.

A slight opalescent glow above his head convinced Tom the hour was near noon. He twisted his neck to look up toward *Annie's* deck, the inaccessible sanctuary several feet above him. The face of a wild-eyed creature was peering down on him from the gunwale.

Ice surged through Tom's veins. He felt the ghost of his granddaughter had returned to taunt him.

"Please forgive me, Rachel," he moaned.

"Tom, Tom, it's me!"

Rachel was crying hysterically as she tugged at his lanyard in an ineffectual effort to lift him aboard.

"I'm frightened, Grandpa, I'm frightened!"

"Rachel," Tom said. "You have to stop the boat!"

Annie's uncharted course through the water had to be aborted, if they had any chance of surviving.

"Let me get you back aboard first," Rachel pleaded, her voice shrill and wailing.

"Rachel," Tom persisted. "There is no time. You have to drop the sails, now!"

Tom listened as Rachel released the mainsail and staysail halyards at the mast pulpit. As *Annie's* heel eased and she came up on her lines, the tension on Tom's lanyard slacked off. He was just beginning to relish the decrease in his discomfort when he dropped deeper into the frigid sea. Tom was now being dragged under the water. With maximum effort, he was able to pull himself up enough to keep his head partially out of the water. He felt that his chest was exploding. He could see that he was now coughing up blood.

As *Annie's* speed through the water slowed, Tom was able to pull himself higher until he was hanging waist deep in the water. Rivulets of scarlet were swirling into the water near *Annie's* hull. Tom sensed a strange indifference to what he was sure was his imminent death.

But Rachel was alive, kneeling on the deck just above his head. He could feel her tugging at the lanyard.

"Get the block and tackle from the life sling," Tom managed.

Tom knew his granddaughter would not be able to get him back aboard unless she could winch him up over the gunwale. Rachel was off to the cockpit to fetch the gear in a flash.

Tom could hear the clacking sound of the tackle on the fiberglass decks as Rachel dragged the gear back to his position. Suddenly she cried out.

"Tom, look!"

Off the port quarter, three dorsal fins were slicing through the water, tracking straight for the boat. Tom's benumbed mind recycled the terrifying lore of sharks. The blood he had spilled into the sea had become a homing device, which had drawn the predators to a quite possibly fatal rendezvous.

"What should I do?" Rachel cried out.

Tom did not feel there was time to rig the block and tackle. In a calm, almost indifferent voice, however, he relayed instructions to his granddaughter.

As they rushed in, Tom felt mesmerized by the sharks. His legs were completely numb, so he had reason to hope there would be little pain. The nearest fin heeled to the side as the lead shark positioned its body to strike. Tom felt a thud. His body was lifted from the water as the animal made contact. As he fell back into the gray water, he expected to the see the water turn crimson, but there was no change. Rachel was scurrying to the base of the mast, frantically rigging the block and tackle rescue system, but Tom was convinced she would be too late.

The first two sharks swept past the boat, both creatures apparently unable to pin Tom to *Annie's* slippery hull. The third animal had veered off and was now bearing straight down on him. Suddenly, the snout and awesome jaws of the shark burst from the murky water. The animal struck the side of *Annie's* hull bluntly with another dull thud, missing Tom by inches. The creature lurched and twisted to the side, trying for a better angle of attack. Instinctively, Tom hammered at its snout with the fist of his useable right arm as the shark tried to impale him to *Annie's* underbody.

Suddenly, Rachel had her arms around her grandfather's neck. He could feel his granddaughter reach down precariously—they were both lost if she bolted from the deck—and then clip the carbine hook of the rescue line to his harness. She seemed to be muttering incoherently.

The sharks were circling for another strike. Tom watched the sleek dorsal fins slicing toward him through the water. He was feeling a sense of apathetic awe for the tenacity of the creatures. But then his sagging body began to rise slowly from the water. The pain in his chest was excruciating, as his full weight fell into the confining straps of the harness, but Rachel was winching him aboard.

Chapter Thirteen

That Tom O'Connor still had legs, that the sharks had missed, that *Annie's* hull had thwarted the predators was alone beyond belief. That Rachel had managed to winch him back aboard was more incredible. That they were both still alive seemed miraculous.

Tom lay quietly atop *Annie's* cabin top. Rachel was cradled at his right shoulder. Between sobs and a nearly hysterical mania, Rachel managed to convey her version of the events of the preceding night.

"I didn't know what hit us, Tom! I thought we might have struck a rock. I went up on deck, but I couldn't find you. Oh, Tom, I thought you had gone overboard.

"You should see what has happened below. All of the instruments are dead, the radios, the radar, even the batteries. I had to put out some fires. I was so scared, I didn't know what to do. I didn't think I'd ever see you again. I didn't think I'd ever see anyone again.

"Let's go home, Grandpa. Please, let's go home!"

Tom tried to think, but coherency came only with difficulty. Yes, they had to go home, but how? Nothing was visible or audible beyond the wall of fog surrounding *Annie*. The danger was still great. There was no way to calculate the *Anna Livia's* position. She had been sailing through a region of oscillating tidal currents and might now be anywhere on the

Gulf of Maine. The treacherous tides of the Grand Manaan Channel or the Bay of Fundy might be drawing them yet to a fatal grounding.

The front was rapidly approaching. Without batteries, the engine could not be started. Even if he were able to reach the hand crank, Tom realized that neither he nor Rachel would be able to turn the heavy diesel over rapidly enough to start it.

Tom grasped his granddaughter's diminutive shoulder and drew her closer.

"You saved my life. You know that, don't you?"

Rachel said nothing. She seemed content with renewed contact with him. They both slept for a time, a consequence of sheer emotional and physical exhaustion.

Tom awoke to find Rachel sitting propped against the mast pulpit watching him. Her face was no longer that of a young girl. A careworn, haggard pair of eyes peered from that face. He had seen that expression once before, when he had picked Rachel up at the convent. Tom berated himself for inflicting such a brutal loss of innocence upon his granddaughter.

Although his chest felt like it was filled with jagged glass, he was gratified to find he had much more strength in his right arm. He was also now able to move his legs.

The time was late afternoon. A strange eerie quiet had descended upon the sea. The soft soughing of the wind in the rigging was gentle, almost harmonious in quality. The sky was overcast, but the fog had dissipated to wispy patches that seemed to waft over the boat like filaments of gossamer cotton.

From his vantage point, Tom could see the swells receding into the distance like the hillocks of a Yorkshire moor. He thought about the ending of *Wuthering Heights*, remembering the quiet sleepers there in the quiet earth. He envied them, for he sensed that the tranquil sea would not remain quiet long.

No land or shoals were in sight and there was no sound of breaking waves. Tom could only hope they were still considerably offshore. The

Anna Livia's best chance to survive the coming storm would be to lie ahull on the open ocean and stand to it under bare poles. He knew Rachel could sail the *Anna Livia* alone if she had to, but taking a heading due west toward the shore would only bring them into greater danger at a time when visibility from the weather might be zero. Although *Annie* was equipped with an emergency inflatable life raft, she was not taking on water and there appeared to be no reason to abandon ship. Tom tried to test his decision to lie ahull for validity, but his mind was apathetic and incapable of any degree of rational deliberation.

A look at the sky confirmed that the storm would be on them soon. Pinnacles of ragged cloud hung inverted from the denser formations above them, a sure sign of violent weather ahead. A steady rain began to fall.

Rachel battened down the sails and then helped get Tom below. He rightly feared pneumonia. Pneumonia is said to be the old man's friend, he wryly reflected. With a great deal of effort, Tom was able to make it to the companionway hatch. Again using the block and tackle, Rachel was able to lower him slowly to the cabin sole. Waves of shaking chills were beginning to buffet Tom's body. He could sense the onset of fever.

Tom lay sweating on the saloon sole, too weak to attempt a bunk. Rachel covered him with one of the sleeping bags and wedged him into position with cushions. He was able to swallow some water and a couple of antibiotic capsules that had been stashed in the first-aid kit. He was sure this was a useless gesture, since the prescription was at least seven years old.

Tom did not want to confront the grave danger he and his granddaughter were in. There were only two possible outcomes to such a precarious situation. The *Anna Livia* would be discovered and saved, or they would flounder on the rocks. Much depended on the direction of the wind and the duration of the heavy weather. A strong nor'easter would drive them down onto the coast of Maine and its innumerable rocks and shoals.

Tom had coached Rachel on the proper use of the flares aboard the now crippled *Anna Livia.* At the sight or sound of an engine in the sky or on the sea, she was prepared to launch a barrage of pyrotechnics.

As his granddaughter was preparing to go topsides to maintain a lookout for ships, Tom became aware of a faint beeping sound coming from the vicinity of the companionway stairs.

"What's that noise?" he mumbled, half deliriously.

Rachel held up, part of the way to the top of the egress ladder.

"That's the radio beacon," she said. "I turned it on this morning, just before I found you, Tom."

"The *EPIRB*?" Tom asked, almost with incredulity. "You turned on the *EPIRB*?"

"You told me I was supposed to do that," Rachel contended, "if I thought we were sinking."

Tom looked at his granddaughter, his eyes stinging with pride.

"What you did was good, Skipper," he managed. "You did exactly the right thing."

"I'll check on you every few minutes," Rachel said, as she demonstrated that the tether of her safety harness was clipped to the cockpit pad eye. Then she bounded through the companionway hatch to stand her first watch.

Tom O'Connor thought about the *EPIRP, Annie's* emergency position indicating radio beacon. If the device was functioning properly, it had been emitting a radio impulse that may have been picked up by now by an aircraft or satellite. The beacon was rated for 72 hours of continuous signal emission and was operating with a self-contained battery that should not have been adversely affected by the lightning strike.

The anticipated storm finally hit the *Anna Livia* and her crew. Tom, often unaware of the tempest raging outside, lay delirious on the cabin sole. His experience of the ensuing 36 hours became a kaleidoscope of visions, punctuated by longer periods of unconsciousness.

Tom felt little fear or panic. Rachel's face, or Anna's, would enter his awareness from the periphery, each of these soothing and reassuring, like the face of the porcelain angel mounted to the bulkhead nearby.

Tom was aware at times of the banshee whine of the wind in the rigging topsides. He imagined the raging sea a battlefield. He misinterpreted the shocks, as *Annie* was buffeted by confused and angry waves, as the explosions of artillery shells falling from a blood-red weeping sky. When he thought the wind might be subsiding to become the soft refrains of music, the gusts would accelerate again as a screaming cacophony, as the blasts tore crests from the building waves outside.

Spawned in the farmlands of Kansas, the weather system had swept with growing fury through the lower Great Lakes, had groaned through the gaps in the upper Appalachian range, and had then descended upon the coast of New England. Throughout the night and then through another day and a night, the storm battered the fishing ports of Maine and it battered the *Anna Livia*, Whiskey, Tango, X-ray 2773, as she floundered on the open waters of the Gulf of Maine.

Only later, would the Coast Guard report winds clocked at 70 knots at Rockport, Camden, Blue Hill, and Tenants Harbor. The storm would leave in its wake moorings torn from the bottom of the ocean and during its rage, three ships would be lost at sea. Sailors would die in that storm, the victims of hubris, and they would join countless other mariners, sailors who had fallen from grace with the sea because they had tested the North Atlantic Ocean one time too often.

Rachel O'Connor stayed with her ship through those two interminable nights. She cranked *Annie's* bilge pump until her shoulders were numb. She lived her baptism under fire on the black North Atlantic. Later, Rachel would speak of that storm softly, with no trace of a child's enthusiasm for an experience she would never choose to live through again.

Throughout the long hours of turbulence, as Rachel, *Annie*, and Tom clung precariously to existence, the *EPIRB* continued to emit signals at 121.5 and 243.0 *MHZ*. Confusion and disorientation reigned in Tom's mind when the *Pequod* finally arrived. The grating whop of the rotor blades seemed to be the flapping wings of a pterodactyl come upon the scene to consume its terrified and helpless prey.

The *Grand Manan* arrived later. The *Anna Livia* was invaded by a swarm of U.S. Coast Guard personnel.

EPILOGUE

Chapter One

The *Grand Manan* towed *Annie* into Southwest Harbor. Rachel was dreadfully worried about Tom, but she dutifully stood to the helm as her boat cleared Cow Ledge. Because the *Anna Livia* was in no danger of sinking, she was placed temporarily on a mooring. Arrangements were later made to move her to the yard of *Hinckley Yachts*, for haul out inspection and necessary repairs. *Hinckley* is located on the southern shore of Southwest Harbor, in nearby Manset.

Tom was medically evacuated to the *Eastern Maine Medical Center* in Bangor. He had been admitted to the hospital with dehydration, pneumonia, multiple rib fractures and a punctured lung. He had also dislocated his left shoulder. Despite the alarming nature of his illness and injuries, his physicians attributed his eventual recovery to his overall good physical conditioning. The hospital staff thought Tom was "one tough old buzzard."

Once Rachel was assured that Tom's condition was stable, she allowed the crew of the *Grand Manan* to treat her to a lobster dinner, with dessert, at *Beal's Lobster* on the pier just across from the Coast Guard Station. She was also taken on a V.I.P. tour of the *Mount Desert Oceanarium*. Rachel enjoyed an afternoon of celebrity as the heroic survivor of an ordeal at sea, while the Station Commander contacted the Maine Department of Social Services for advice about what to do with his new charge.

And so, Rachel, *Annie*, and Tom were safe. After nearly three months on the run, the renegade O'Connors and their ship were firmly in the hands of the authorities.

Rachel next saw Tom six days later, when Margaret Malone—the social worker assigned to her case—drove her to Bangor for a visit. Rachel had been in daily telephone contact with Tom, providing him with updates on *Annie's* repairs. Mrs. Malone had also been in contact on their behalf with Sheila Ingrahm, who still represented the State of Michigan's interest in Rachel's case. Mrs. Malone had been able to postpone Rachel's immediate extradition to the Midwest by assuming personal custody of her young charge. Rachel O'Connor had the dubious distinction of being a ward of *two* States of the union at the same time.

The charge nurse had no sooner escorted Rachel into her grandfather's room, when the youngster stopped dead in her tracks, her eyes blinking with disbelief. She took one look at Tom and then nearly collapsed on the floor, a horrendous belly laugh rumbling out of her mouth. Rachel had to be warned by the nurse that she was in a hospital, as she pranced around the room, slapping her knees and squealing with hilarious delight.

"Look at you, Tom!" Rachel managed, with a guffaw. "You look terrific! I hardly recognized you."

Tom's face turned crimson to the tips of his ears. He emitted a nervous cough and gestured toward the next bed with his thumb, encouraging Rachel to regain her composure, but she persisted.

"You look *handsome*, Tom!" she declared. "I can't believe it's you!"

Rachel raced over to her grandfather's bedside and planted a loud smacker on his forehead. Then she stepped back, surveying his profile from several angles.

"Wait till Margaret gets a load of you," she said, embellishing the remark with a wolfish whistle. "You better watch out, Tom. Mrs. Malone is a widow."

Rachel's commentary was interrupted by another round of raucous laughter.

"I told her you looked like an old mountain goat!" she added gleefully.

Tom's hair had been closely cropped, shampooed, and combed. His beard and moustache had been neatly trimmed and sculpted. Even he had to admit that these ministrations lent a certain debonair flair to his more distinguished appearance. His earring was nowhere in evidence.

"Marjorie, my morning star there, suggested the overhaul," Tom explained, gesturing toward the charge nurse, who was smiling back at him with a rakish grin on her face.

"And quite an improvement, I might add," Marjorie suggested.

"I'll say!" Rachel agreed.

Tom's transformed face was bearing a sheepish expression.

"From what your Mrs. Malone had told me, Skipper, my greatest legal battle is imminent," he said. "I don't suppose a more professional appearance will be a liability."

"You'll knock them dead, Tom," Rachel said with assurance.

Tom looked longingly at the confident gleam in his granddaughter's eyes. He was by no means as assured as Rachel of the outcome of her custody hearing.

"Pull up a chair," he said softly. "We need to have a little talk."

Marjorie charitably left Tom and his granddaughter to themselves. Rachel sat down. For a few moments, Tom said nothing.

"You know, Skipper," he finally began. "I have done some dreadfully stupid things in my life. Not the least was almost getting us both killed. But the stupidest of all was allowing myself to become selfish after I lost your grandmother. That selfishness cost me four invaluable years I could have spent with you and your mother."

At the reference to Claire, Rachel looked down, suddenly interested—it appeared—in her hands.

"The second dumbest thing I ever did was to run off with you the way I did," Tom continued.

Rachel looked up sharply. Her eyes were glistening.

"You mean you didn't really want me to live with you?" she asked tentatively.

Tom held out his arms. Rachel was clinging to his neck in seconds.

"I shouldn't have brought you out here to the boat!" he said, disparagingly. "I should have gotten a suit, cut my silly hair, and played the game. Had I done that, we wouldn't be in all of this trouble."

"Mrs. Malone says there is a chance they won't put me in a foster home," Rachel suggested. She had regained some of her exuberance.

"Well, it is good of your Mrs. Malone to say that," Tom said. "I just want you to know that I'm going to fight like the devil to keep you," he added.

"I have decided that once we get this legal business behind us, I'm going to buy a house, if that's O.K. with you. Maybe we'll get an old sea captain's place, with turrets and lots of windows overlooking the sea, in one of the harbor towns here in Maine. We'll pick a place with good schools where you can have tons of friends. We'll keep *Annie*, of course. I know some neat summer anchorages I'm sure you'll like."

Rachel buried her face in her grandfather's neck.

"I love you, Grandpa," she said.

"They say a picture is worth a thousand words."

This last pronouncement—expressed with a hint of a brogue—had come from the doorway to Tom O'Connor's room. He looked up to confront a woman in her mid-fifties. She was dressed in a business suit. She immediately reminded Tom of someone—the Irish actress who had done so many of the plays of Eugene O'Neill—but he could not recall the actress's name. The woman standing in the doorway had a careworn, much lived in face. Her face was earthy, but Tom O'Connor found it not at all unattractive.

The speaker entered the room, extending a hand to the patient.

"I'm Margaret Malone," she said, greeting Tom warmly, as she approached his bedside.

Chapter Two

After his brief and awkward introduction to Margaret Malone—an experience Tom felt he had bungled badly—Rachel and her guardian returned to nearby Bucksport, where Mrs. Malone was living. Tom remained hospitalized for an additional three days following Rachel's visit. His convalescence would continue following his discharge from the hospital in a spare room in Margaret Malone's home.

Tom was nonplussed by his reaction to Margaret Malone. When he tried to analyze his unpolished reactions to this sophisticated social worker, he cited lingering guilt over the way he had foolishly handled the situation with Rachel. He also admitted his general awkwardness interacting with adults. As a virtual recluse for over four years, Tom was as rusty as a neglected steel hull when it came to casual conversation, especially with women.

Most of what Tom learned about Margaret Malone came from Rachel, tidbits he managed to glean while feigning indifference about the social worker's life. Margaret Malone was living in Bucksport alone. Her two children were grown and had apparently joined an exodus of youth out of Maine in search of better opportunities elsewhere. According to Rachel, Margaret Malone did not talk much about her late husband, offering only something vague about an accident at sea some years in the past.

"Does she ever ask anything about me?" Tom asked during a phone conversation with Rachel just before his discharge from *EMMC*. "Just out of curiosity?" he quickly added.

"Not much," Rachel informed her crestfallen grandfather, "but she does seem awfully interested in Grandma, though."

In the meantime, Tom conducted a form of shuttle diplomacy with Sheila Ingrahm via long-distance telephone. Ms Ingrahm felt confident that the State of Michigan would not pursue criminal charges against Tom for the unlawful transport of a minor across State lines. She was by no means optimistic about the outcome of Rachel's now long delayed custody hearing.

Serious, probably fatal, questions about Tom O'Connor's judgement and sense of responsibility had obviously been raised by his conduct. The State might insist upon foster home placement for Rachel, as a temporary measure, while a formal evaluation of Mr. O'Connor's suitability as a guardian was determined.

Tom could imagine, as he spoke with her on the telephone, Sheila Ingrahm's recollection of his appearance. He was tempted, but then thought better of mentioning his recent cosmetic transformation. Tom was hoping to use the overhaul of his locks and whiskers as a trump card when he met with Ms. Ingrahm's again.

On the day of Tom's discharge from the hospital, Margaret Malone graciously agreed to pick him up and drive him to his temporary abode at her home in Bucksport. Mrs. Malone arrived at the hospital at 11:00 A.M. with her excited charge in tow. Tom, irritated at being transported down to the lobby in a wheelchair, made a macho display of strength—hardly disguised as for Margaret Malone's benefit—as he entered the social worker's car. He and his healing rib cage would regret the gesture later.

Because of Tom's punctured lung, his physicians at *EMMC* told him he would be wise not to travel by car or by air for at least a month following his injury. Sheila Ingrahm was able to lock in a spot on the court docket one month to the day after Tom had been hurt.

Since neither he nor Rachel felt up to another automobile trip to the Midwest, Tom reluctantly decided to fly out to Michigan. Although it is possible to get a connecting flight out of Bangor, he wheedled a promise from Margaret Malone to drive the travelers down to *Logan International Airport* in Boston, when the time came to leave Maine. There appeared little wisdom—he speculated—in pushing his luck with multiple takeoffs and landings.

During the 2½ weeks Tom spent on the mend in Bucksport, he had not felt much like venturing very far afield. Other than slow walks into town for needed exercise, he remained at Margaret's home, catching up on some reading and planning his strategy for the court battle. Just after Labor Day, Rachel started school in Bucksport.

Because of Mrs. Malone's busy work schedule, she and Tom did not have many opportunities to get to know each other well. Both had aspects of their respective pasts that remained difficult to talk about freely. The interchanges he did have with Margaret became increasingly pleasurable and anticipated by Tom, but he was plagued by doubts that she felt the same.

Finally, the time came for Tom and Rachel to fly to Michigan. The drive down to *Logan* turned out not to be direct. Tom induced Margaret to include a "short side trip" down to Southwest Harbor via Ellsworth, even though this would take them in a direction opposite to the normal route from Bucksport to Boston.

To her credit, Margaret Malone sensed that Tom was in need—on this, the eve of the most important court battle in his professional life—of the inner strength that he could only derive from contact with his boat. As a Mainer, Mrs. Malone understood such needs. She had lived and worked with lobstermen and sailors most of her life. She knew that the bond between a mariner and an inanimate ship is often able to transcend human relationships, to assume a poignancy that can border on the sacred.

From his position in the back seat of Margaret Malone's sedan, Tom watched the silhouettes of pine trees rush past his window. In his mind's eye, he was visualizing the port towns and harbors of coastal Maine that dotted the shoreline a few miles away. The weather was brisk on this late summer day. The wind was coming out of the west, a good day for flying rags.

Tom was reticent, his mood taciturn, his sporadic conversation constrained. For the first time in weeks, he sensed Anna's presence. Now and then, he had to check the temptation to speak to her.

Rachel—from the passenger's side of the front seat—was regaling Mrs. Malone with additional details about the odyssey to Nova Scotia. The diversionary junket passed quickly, the party arriving in Southwest Harbor shortly after eleven.

Rachel proposed an early lunch at *Beal's*. Tom toyed with a bucket of steamers, while the lobsters the two females had ordered—and hypnotized at Rachel's insistence—became a gourmet's delight. Tom seemed unable to muster much of an appetite.

"Why don't you drive over to the yard, Tom," Mrs. Malone suggested gently, restraining Rachel's incipient protest with a nudge beneath the table. "If you take it slow, I'm sure you'll be alright. You can come back for Rachel and me later."

Tom looked at Margaret Malone with an expression of gratitude. Taking her car keys, he drove out to the *Hinckley* yard in Manset at the other side of the harbor.

He found her shored up and settled in for the coming winter. A *Hans Christian* cannot really hold a candle to a *Hinckley*, but as he compared her lines with the two *Bermuda 40s* in the yard, Tom was sure *Annie* was the most beautiful yacht in Southwest Harbor. He had not seen her in dry dock in several years. As he walked up to her bow, she looked sad, like a great sea bird grounded with clipped, but still iridescent wings.

Tom approached and gently caressed her hull.

"It's good to see you, Anna," he mumbled beneath his breath.

There seemed so much more he wanted to say, but the emotion of being there alone with her once again checked his speech. He said nothing more, busying himself by scrounging around for a boarding ladder.

Finding a rickety object in the last stages of decay beneath the hulk of an old trawler, Tom tested the rungs for stability. Then he boarded the *Anna Livia*, as he had done with his wife the first time they had realized that she actually belonged to them, so many years before.

Conditions were cold topsides in the stiff wind making out to sea from the surrounding hills, but Tom hardly noticed. He removed the pedestal cover, liberating *Annie's* helm. He sat at her helmsman's seat, gripping her wheel as he had done so many times before. He traced her sheer line as it rushed gracefully port and starboard to completion at her bow. Memories came crashing into his brain like the waves battering the ancient rocks nearby.

She had been so *good* for him all of her life. The wind and the scenes before him stung Tom's eyes. How very good she had been for him. He saw her as she had appeared on the evening they had met, on the night she had entered his life. Standing in a doorway with the light silhouetting her figure, her body had been girded by a soft golden glow. He had never seen anyone so beautiful, not before, not since. Instantly, in that magical moment, the soft, flowing murmur of her being had entwined itself about his heart, where it would remain forever.

They were at sail, the three of them at sail again on a moonlit, silver sea. *Annie* was working to weather in a perfect wind, a gracefully strong and vibrantly living creature. They were together, the three of them, sharing an unspeakable perfection and completion. How could something so beautiful possibly end?

Suddenly, Tom felt very cold. He shivered in the stiff Atlantic coastal wind. He stood up and took one last, longing look at his aging boat. At that moment, she seemed to be peering back at him hauntingly through her veneer of finery, from a hollow shell of remembrance of past glories, now irretrievably lost. For the first time, Tom grasped the sad truth that he would never see her again.

Tom slowly climbed back down the ladder. He stowed the rickety object where he had found it beneath the old trawler. He walked back to Margaret Malone's sedan and drove back over to *Beal's*.

"Tom!" Rachel cried, when she saw her grandfather walking toward her and Mrs. Malone. Recognizing him, she bolted off to greet him.

"Aren't we going to show *Annie* to Margaret?" she asked, when she reached his side.

Tom encircled his granddaughter in his arm and led her to the spot where Margaret Malone stood waiting.

"Maybe another time," he said, almost inaudibly. "We have to go now."

The trio retraced their steps in silence to Margaret's car. As the road wound out of Southwest Harbor, Tom resisted his impulse to look back. Rachel had resumed her animated commentary from the front seat.

"Next summer, we'll take you sailing, Margaret. It's easy to learn, really. We'll both teach you."

Tom had been staring blankly out of the window. He happened to look up toward the rearview mirror, where his eyes met those of Margaret Malone. She was watching him intently at intervals as she drove.

"Tom will teach you marlinspiking, Margaret," Rachel was saying. "That's the science of tying knots, but Tom calls it *merlinspiking*, because the ropes are alive and do weird things by magic and sorcery."

Tom scrutinized the eyes framed in the mirror. He felt that he had never seen such eyes before. They were eyes filled with a great deal of sadness and feeling. They had obviously witnessed much pain. Tom was convinced that Margaret Malone was reading a similar message in his eyes as well.

"When do you think we'll launch her in the spring, Tom?"

Tom did not respond to his granddaughter's question immediately. He was preoccupied, his mind involved with many things. He was thinking about Rachel and *Annie* and he was savoring the sudden conviction that he would win the custody battle no matter how long that took and that they *would* sail together—he, and Rachel, and Maggie Malone. Tom felt he would be returning to useful employment again, as a volunteer perhaps, and that he would learn the art of merlinspiking from Maggie Malone. He could sense that his life would be full, complete, and rich once again.

"What?" he muttered.

"Tell Margaret she can sail with us, Tom!" Rachel insisted.

Margaret Malone redirected her eyes from the road to the mirror once again. Tom O'Connor answered her penetrating gaze from across a narrowing chasm of lost time and mutual pain, and said "yes, oh yes," to Maggie Malone's intriguing Irish eyes.

The End

Glossary of Nautical Terms

Abaft: Behind or toward the stern of a boat.
Abeam: To one side of a boat, at a right angle to the line extending from the bow to the stern (fore and aft line). "The lighthouse lies abeam."
Adrift: Floating free in the water.
Aft, after: To the rear, at or near the stern of a boat.
Aground: Stuck against the sea bottom.
Alee: On the sheltered side or away from the direction from which the wind is blowing.
Aloft: Above the decks. To go aloft on a sailboat is usually to climb the mast.
Amidships: In the center of a boat.
Anchor rode: A long rope or chain used to connect a boat to its anchor.
Astern: The direction toward the stern of a boat, or beyond the stern.
Aweigh: Off the bottom, said of an anchor being raised from the bottom.

Backstay: A stainless steel line running from the masthead to the stern. Part of the *standing rigging* of a sailboat.
Backwind: To deliberately hold a sail into the wind so that it acts as a brake. Back winding the mainsail is often used to slow the forward progress of a sailboat when docking or anchoring.

Bare poles: Said of a sailboat on the water with no sails flying and usually adrift.

Barograph: An instrument that continuously records atmospheric pressure, useful in predicting weather.

Beam: The width of a boat's hull or the direction at a right angle to the centerline of a vessel. "The lighthouse lies broad on the beam."

Beam ends, to be on her beam ends: A dangerous position when a *broaching* boat lies on its side in the water and can easily be swamped or sunk. A sailboat carrying too much sail for the prevailing wind strength can be "knocked on its beam ends."

Beam reach: Sailing with the wind blowing at a right angle to the boat's fore and aft line.

Bearing: The direction of an object (another boat, buoy, lighthouse etc) from an observer.

Bear off, bear away: To turn a vessel away from the wind.

Beat, to beat, beating: Sailing toward a destination from where the wind is coming. To do this a sailboat must make a zigzag course (a series of *tacks*) keeping the wind about 45° off the bow on each *tack.*

Beaufort Scale of Wind Force: See *Wind, force of*

Belay: To make a rope secure by winding it around a belaying pin or cleat.

Below, go below: The interior of a boat beneath the decks, or to move to that area.

Berth, quarter berth, bunk: A place to sleep on a boat.

Bight: The middle of a rope, a loop in a rope, or an indentation in a shoreline.

Bilge: The lowest point in the interior of a boat's hull where incoming water will usually collect.

Bilge pump: A mechanical device, powered by electricity or by hand, used to empty the water from a boat's bilge.

Boom: A spar attached at a right angle to a boat's mast. The lower part (foot) of a sail is often attached to the boom.

Bow: The forward or front end of a boat.
Bowline: A useful knot used to make a loop at the end of a rope.
Bowsprit: A spar or platform extending from the bow of a boat. On some sailboats, the headstay is attached to the bowsprit. One or more anchors are often stowed on a bowsprit.
Bring about (see also Come About and Tack): To steer a sailboat's bow through the wind when beating, tacking, or sailing to weather.
Broach, broaching: The sudden, unplanned, and often dangerous turning of a vessel so its hull is broadside to the waves and/or wind. A vessel in this position can be swamped or overturned in the water.
Broad reach: Sailing with the wind aft of the beam, but not directly astern, usually a very comfortable sailing condition.
Bulkhead: A transverse wall set into a boat's hull that creates its inner compartments or rooms.
Buoy: A floating aid to navigation that marks the limits of a channel or some danger, such as a rock or shoal.

Can: A cylindrical buoy, usually painted green and marked with an odd number.
Cap rail: Trim, often of teak, mounted to the top of a boat's gunwhale.
Carbine hook: A metal fitting on a safety tether that can be rapidly engaged or released.
Canoe stern: A vessel with similar curves in the bow and stern.
Cast off: To loosen all mooring lines in preparation for departure.
Ceiling: The inside lining of a boat's hull.
Cleat: A fitting to which lines are attached.
Close-hauled: Sailing as close as possible to the wind.
Cockpit: Space on the exterior of a boat for the crew to occupy.
Come about: To tack, to change direction in reference to the wind when the boat is trying to reach a place from where the wind is blowing.
Companionway: A hatch or entrance from the outside decks to the interior cabin of a boat.

Course: The direction in which a vessel is steered, often expressed in degrees of a compass.

Cutter: A sailboat with a single mast, a mainsail, and two sails forward of the mast, usually a staysail and a jib or genoa (see *Mainsail, Staysail, Jib, Genoa*) or a fast power driven boat, a Coast Guard Cutter, for example.

Dead ahead, dead astern: Directions exactly in front of or behind a vessel, respectively.

Dinghy: A small boat used to transport crew and supplies to or from a larger vessel. See also, tender.

Ditch, the Ditch: A colloquial term among East Coast boaters for the Atlantic Ocean.

Double-ender (see *canoe stern*)*:* A boat design in which the stern resembles the bow in configuration.

Douse: To lower a sail.

Downwind: A direction to leeward, away from the wind.

Draft: The vertical direction from the waterline to the lowest point of a vessel's hull. The minimum depth of water in which a vessel will float.

Ease: To let out a line under full control.

EPIRB or Emergency Position Indicating Radio Beacon: A small transmitter using a standard frequency to alert authorities of a distress situation and to lead rescuers to the scene.

Fender: A cushioning device hung between a boat and a float, pier, or other boat.

Fetch: To sail a course that will clear a buoy or danger. Also, the distance across the water the wind has been blowing.

Fix: The determination of the exact position of a vessel by any means.

Flasher: A light that blinks on and off at some predetermined sequence.

Fo'c'sle (forecastle): A compartment in the extreme bow of a boat.

Following sea: A situation in which waves approach a boat from the stern.
Foot: The bottom edge of a sail.
Force two-eight wind: see *Wind, force of*
Fore: Located at or toward the front of a boat.
Fore and aft: From bow to stern, from front to back in a line parallel to the keel of a boat.
Forecabin: A compartment in the front of a boat as opposed to an aft cabin, which is nearer the stern.
Forecastle (see *Fo'c'sle*)
Foredeck: The forward part of the exterior of a boat near the bow.
Forepeak: The extreme forward compartment of a boat, usually used for stowage.
Forestay: A line, usually of stainless steel, running from near the top of the mast to the foredeck (see also *Headstay*). Part of the *standing rigging* of a sailboat.
Forestaysail or staysail: A sail attached to the forestay, usually smaller than a jib (which is usually attached to the headstay). A modern single-masted sailboat with a staysail is referred to as a *cutter* or as *cutter-rigged.*
Forward: The direction to the front of a boat, toward the bow.
Furl, furling, to furl: The process of folding, rolling, or gathering a sail to make its area smaller. Often done on a sailboat as the wind increases in force. A similar term is *reefing.*

Galley: The kitchen aboard a boat.
Gel coat: The standard smooth outer finish of a fiberglass boat.
Genoa, genny: A headsail or jib so large that it overlaps the mast. Provides great wind gathering power to a sailboat.
Ground tackle: The anchor, anchor rode, shackles, and other gear used in making a boat fast to the sea bottom.
Gunwale: The upper edge of the side of a boat, which projects above the deck.

Hail: A call to a ship or boat.
Halyard: A line or rope used to hoist a sail or spar.
Hard over: All the way in one direction, as a tiller or wheel.
Harden: To haul in or tighten a line.
Hatch: An opening in the deck of a ship giving access to the area below.
Head, heads: The upper corner of a triangular sail. Also, the toilet aboard a boat, either the fixture or the entire compartment.
Heading: The direction in which a boat is pointed at any given moment.
Headsail: Any of several sails set forward of the mast. (see *staysail, headsail, jib, genoa, storm jib*).
Head seas: Waves coming from the direction in which a boat is heading.
Headstay: A line, usually of stainless steel, running from the top of the mast to the bow, to which headsails are attached. Part of the *standing rigging* of a sailboat.
Headway: Forward progress of a vessel through the water.
Heaving to; hove to: Setting the sails so the boat rides easy in the waves and makes little headway, usually done in a storm or waiting situation.
Heavy weather: Stormy, windy weather with rough water, high seas, and possible discomfort or danger.
Heel, heeling: To tip or lean to one side, a normal situation for a sailboat, if not excessive.
Helm: The tiller, wheel, or other steering mechanism on a boat.
Hook: A term for the anchor of a boat.

Iron jib: A derisive term for the engine of a sailboat. Sailors who are purists hate to "fire up the iron jib," which implies they must motor rather than sail.

Jacklines: Safety ropes running the length of a sailboat's decks, usually on either side, to which safety harnesses can be clipped.
Jib: A triangular sail, usually attached to a *headstay*. If large enough to overlap the mast, a jib is often called a *Genoa*, or *Genny*.

Jibe: To change direction when sailing with the wind aft, so the wind comes onto the opposite quarter and the boom swings over to the opposite side of the boat. When done without careful control of the situation, this can be a dangerous maneuver.

Keel: The main structural component, the backbone of a boat, running fore and aft.

Ketch: A two-masted sailboat in which the after mast (mizzen mast) is shorter than the forward main mast. The mizzen mast on a ketch is placed forward of the rudder post. See also *Yawl*

Knot: A unit of speed, one nautical mile per hour. Also, a general term for a hitch or tie in a line.

Lazarette: A small storage compartment.

Leech: The trailing edge of a triangular sail.

Lee rails: Devices to prevent objects on shelves from falling out as a boat moves through the water.

Leeward: Away from the direction the wind is blowing, on the protected side, downwind.

Leeway: The sliding of a vessel off course in the direction (to the *lee* or to *leeward*) to which the wind is blowing.

Lie ahull: A condition in which a boat drifts in the water under neither engine nor sail power. Often done as a survival tactic in a severe storm.

Lifelines: Plastic covered wire ropes running along the sides of a boat's deck to keep crew from falling overboard.

Locker: A storage place or closet aboard a boat.

Luff: The forward leading edge of a triangular sail. To deliberately steer a sailboat into the wind, to momentarily take power from its sails, as in the expression "to luff in a puff."

Mainsail: The major sail that flies behind the mainmast of a sailboat.

Marlinspiking: The art of using ropes for practical or decorative purposes aboard a boat.

Mast: A vertical spar, the main support of the sailing rig of a sailboat.

Midships: Location near the center of a vessel measured either from side to side or fore and aft.

Mizzen mast: In a ketch or yawl, the smaller aftermost mast, that sets behind the mainmast. The mizzen sail is set on the mizzen mast.

Moored: Anchored or tied to a mooring, pier, or wharf.

Mooring: A set of permanent tackle consisting of a heavy block of concrete on the bottom, chain, and a mooring buoy to which a boat may tie up in a harbor. Moorings are often for rent in popular harbors.

Nun: A cylindrical buoy, tapering toward the top, typically painted red and marked with an even number.

Neap tide: One occurring with the moon at half phase. The range (rise and fall of the water) of a neap tide is smaller than that of a *spring tide.*

Nautical mile: 6076.12 feet, which equals one minute of latitude on a nautical chart.

Pad Eye: A strong ring firmly attached to a boat's cockpit or other location to which gear, often the tether of a safety harness, can be attached.

Painter: A towline or tie up line for a small boat, such as a dinghy.

Passage: One leg of a voyage.

Pay out: To release a line in a controlled manner.

Pedestal: A base upon which a compass, wheel or helm is mounted.

Pinching: Sailing so close to the wind, the boat is in danger of stalling. Pinching is used for short periods of time to reach a destination upwind without tacking.

Port: Left, as the side of a boat when looking toward the bow. A direction to the left side of a boat, for example to "turn to port." An opening in the side of a vessel for light or ventilation. An area on the shore having facilities for handling or maintaining vessels.

Port tack: A sailing vessel with the wind coming from the left or port side is said to be on a port tack.

Pulpit: A railing for support at the bow (*bow pulpit*) or at the mast (*mast pulpit*).

Punt: a small vessel with squared off ends, usually propelled by oars or a pole.

Pushpit: A railing for support at the stern of a vessel, similar to a bow pulpit.

Quarter: Either side of a vessel from amidships to the stern.

Quartering sea: Following seas coming toward the quarter of a vessel on either side.

Quay: A structure, often of masonry or concrete, at the water's edge where vessels can tie up, load, or unload cargo.

Rag bagger: A common term for a sailor, as opposed to a "stinker potter," often applied to a power boater.

Rail down: A sailboat in a stiff wind and sometimes with too much sail for the conditions, such that she is heeling far enough to put her rails in or near the water. Sailing rail down is often a thrilling experience for sailors, but the practice might not be prudent in all situations.

Reach, reaching: Sailing with the wind at an angle to the bow. On a *close reach*, the wind is about half way between the bow and the beam. On a *beam reach*, the wind is on the beam. On a *broad reach*, the wind is aft of the beam.

Reef: To shorten the area of a sail by rolling the sail on a spar or stay (also called *furling*) or by tying in reef points. An underwater barrier made of rock or coral.

Reef knot or *square knot:* A knot used to tie in a reef.

Reef points: Tie lines placed at intervals horizontally on a sail and used to reduce sail area when they are tied around the foot of the sail and the boom.

Rigging: Standing rigging is semi-permanent once set up, usually made of stainless steel wire, and is used to support the mast and sails. Depending on function, elements of the standing rigging may be called *stays*, or *shrouds*. *Running rigging* refers to ropes continually adjusted to hoist, douse, or trim sails. Elements of running rigging include *halyards* and *sheets*.

Rock awash: A rock lying just below the surface of the water that waves wash over. A very dangerous obstruction.

Rode: Anchor line, made of rope, chain, or a combination of the two.

Rogue or rogue wave: A wave larger than usual that can break, bringing water aboard a boat without warning.

Run: Sailing with the wind directly astern. A dangerous point of sail if the main is flying, because the boom can be accidentally thrown from side to side (accidental *jibe*). *To run before the wind* is to sail with the wind aft of a boat.

Saloon: The main cabin or interior compartment on a boat.

Saint Elmo's fire: A rare atmospheric phenomenon in which a greenish glow appears surrounding the top of a mast during an electrical storm, often in advance of a lightning strike.

Schooner: A sail boat with more than one mast, in which the forward mast is smaller than the mainmast, or in which all of the masts are of the same height. Examples are three-masted or four-masted schooners. Schooners were an important part of the New England fishing fleet in the days before the arrival of the steam engine. Windjammers are often schooners.

Scud roll: A churning horizontal cloud formation in advance of a rapidly approaching storm.

Scuppers: Drain holes on the deck or in the cockpit.

Self tailing winch: A winch with a device attached that holds the line being hauled firmly. A self tailing set up allows a sailor to operate the winch with only one hand

Sheer, sheer line: The curvature of a boat's deck when viewed from the side.

Sheet: A line, part of the running rigging of a sailboat, used to control the movement of a sail to the side (*jib sheet*) or to control the movement of a boom (*main sheet*) or other spar.

Shoal: An area of shallow water, because of a rock, reef, or other underwater obstruction, extremely hazardous to navigation.

Shroud: Part of the *standing rigging*, usually running on either side of a mast.

Slip: An area in a marina where a boat can dock and have access to the shore.

Sloop: A sailing vessel with a single mast, a mainsail, and a single headsail.

Sole: The floor of a cabin or cockpit.

Spars: Masts, booms, gaffs, or poles used in a sailboat's rigging.

Spring tide: Tide occurring when the moon is full or new. Not related to the season of the year. At the time of a spring tide, the high tide is higher, the low tide is lower, and the range (total rise and fall of the water) are greater than at the time of a *neap tide.*

Squall: A sudden, violent windstorm. A line of squalls often accompanies the advance of a cold front.

Square knot: Another name for a reef knot, used for tying two lines together or for making the area of a sail smaller during *reefing.*

Stanchion: A vertical pole mounted along the outer edge of a boat's deck to which life lines are mounted.

Standing rigging: See *Rigging*

Starboard tack: A sailing vessel with the wind coming from the right or starboard side is said to be on a starboard tack.

Stateroom: Sleeping quarters on a ship for a guest, captain, or owner.

Stay: Part of the *standing rigging* of a sailboat used to support a mast in the fore and aft direction. Examples are the *Headstay, Forestay,* and *Backstay*

Staysail: A foresail that is set between the mast and the jib. On a sailboat with a single mast, the presence of a staysail defines the boat as a *cutter* or *cutter rigged.*

Stern: The rear or after portion of a boat.

Swell: A long, large wave that does not crest or break.

Tack: Each leg of a zigzag course sailed into the wind or downwind. Depending on the side of the boat the wind is on, the designation is *Port* or *Starboard Tack.* The front bottom corner of a triangular sail.

Tacking, to Tack: Sailing maneuver in which the direction of the boat is shifted to bring the wind on the other side. Sailing to alternate tacks is often necessary when a sailboat is trying to make a destination directly upwind. This process is also called *Beating or slogging to weather.*

Tackle: A combination of blocks and lines giving mechanical advantage, such as *ground tackle* using during anchoring.

Tender: A small boat accompanying a yacht used to transport crew, gear, or supplies. Also known as a *Dinghy.*

Tidal current: The horizontal flow of water caused by the rise and fall of the tide. Flow from the ocean due to a rising tide is called a flood current; flow back to the ocean due to a falling tide is called an ebb or ebbing current. The direction of a tidal current at a given point is influenced greatly by the features of a coastline. Without care, tidal currents can set a boat dangerously off course.

Tides: The rise and fall of the ocean water caused by the effects of the sun and the moon.

Tide tables: A publication giving the times of high and low tides, the range of the tide, and information about tidal currents in various locations.

Topsides: On deck, as opposed to below deck. On a boat, one may *go below* or *come topsides.*

Track: The path of a vessel over the water from one location to another.

Traffic Separation Zone or Scheme: A plan by which vessels in congested areas agree to use one way lanes to reduce risk of collision. A small boat must use extreme caution when crossing such a zone and be on constant lookout for large tankers.
Trim or Tune: To set sails to optimum effect by adjusting sheets or other rigging lines.
Trough: Depression between two waves. Also, an expression applying to low atmospheric pressure, as in a storm.

Underway: A vessel not at anchor, aground, or made fast to the shore.
Upwind: To the windward of any point of reference.

Vessel: Any moving and floating craft, such as a boat, ship, or barge.
VHF radio: A Very High Frequency communication device, the common "ship-to-shore" radio used on most boats.

Way: Movement of a vessel through the water. *To get underway* means to initiate movement; *to take all way off* is to stop nearly dead in the water.
Waypoint: Some fixed location (the position of a buoy or a set of latitude and longitude coordinates) along a passage through the water.
Weather, to weather: General term for the meteorological conditions at a given time in a given place The direction from where the wind is blowing.
Weigh: To raise an anchor in preparation for departure.
Wharf: A structure parallel to the shoreline for docking vessels.
Wheel: Steering wheel of a vessel.
Whitecaps: Visible white crests of breaking waves, usually indicating a wind speed of at least 10 knots.
Winch, to winch: A device, mounted on a deck or spar used to haul in a line.
Wind, force of: By observing the size and characteristics of waves, sailors estimate the force or speed of the wind. The system used for doing so is called the *Beaufort Scale of Wind Force.* Some examples are as follows:

Force 2 wind: light breeze, about 5 knots, with small non-breaking waves, no whitecaps.

Force 3 wind: gentle breeze, about 10 knots, with scattered whitecaps.

Force 4 wind: moderate breeze, about 15 knots, waves to 3 ft, numerous white caps.

Force 5 wind: fresh breeze, about 20 knots, waves 3-6 ft, many white caps, some spray.

Force 6 wind: strong breeze, about 25 knots, waves 6-12 ft, white caps everywhere, wind heard in rigging.

Force 7 wind: near gale, about 30 knots, waves 12-18 ft, white foam from breaking waves begins to blow in streaks on the surface of the water.

Force 8 wind: a full gale, about 35 knots, waves may exceed 20 ft.

Windlass: A special form of winch, usually used to haul in an anchor rode.

Windward: The direction from which the wind is blowing.

Yacht: A pleasure boat. The idea of size, luxury, or beauty is often implied by this term.

Yawl: A two-masted sailboat in which the after mast (mizzen mast) is shorter than the forward main mast. The mizzen mast on a yawl is placed behind of the rudder post. See also *Ketch*

About the Author

Paul Seifert, M.D. is a semi-retired physician who devoted his professional career to medical education. He currently resides in Petoskey, a small town on Little Traverse Bay in the northwest corner of the lower peninsula of the State of Michigan.

Dr. Seifert's long-standing interest in creative writing has led to several publications.

"Cowboy O'Rourke and the Big Brass Band," is a novel excerpt published in *The Third Coast: Contemporary Michigan Fiction*. This story, in addition to three other published short stories, "Grenadine," "The Blues Singer," and "The Transformation," are available on Dr. Seifert's web site (www.seifertpaul-md.com).

Paul Seifert's first published novel, *The Man Who Could Read Minds*, is currently out of print, but copies can be obtained by special order at Amazon.com.

Rachel & Annie is Dr. Seifert's second published novel. *Annie*, one of the title characters, is a 38-foot sailboat. Paul Seifert and his wife lived on the boat for eight years and sailed to many of the locations in Maine and Nova Scotia described in the novel.

Printed in the United States
2031